Fly

Francesca

Fly

by Venera Concetta

ISBN: 978-0-9945307-6-9

Book and Cover design by Rainbow Works Pty Ltd.

Published in Australia by Rainbow Works Pty Ltd.

First Edition: October 2020

DISCLAIMER

This book is an artistic work of fiction and, except in the case of historical fact, any resemblance to actual persons, living or dead, is purely coincidental. Any references to specific cultures and cultural practices are reasonably held, made in good faith and are an expression of genuine belief made by the author in the distribution of this artistic work.

To every woman and man, past, present, and

future, who dreams of flying high

There is no greater agony than bearing

an untold story inside you.

Maya Angelou (1928 — 2014)

Chapter 1

"My father died yesterday," I replied.

The silence shattered by these words could no longer be stitched back together.

These words that fell from my lips did not feel like my truth; they were someone else's truth, from someone else's life.

"Oh, I'm so sorry," replied Wendy.

"You couldn't have known."

My hand groped the receiver. I didn't want her sympathy.

Part of me was angry. What are you apologising for? I wanted to scream.

The sound of my fingers tapping on the table filled the void in the room, in my head.

"It was a relief actually when he finally went," I said, the words an unexpected release from the obligation I felt to neatly manicure the truth.

"Oh!" gasped Wendy on the other end of the phone.

I looked down at the half-filled page of the blue-lined writing pad, at the letter I had started to write. As I read and reread the words, I slid into a trance, the repetition of the words mesmerising me.

"Write a letter to your mother," my therapist had said. "Don't send it though. It will be cathartic and healing for you."

Where should I start? How should I start? I wondered for a long time.

One day, the thought occurred to me: *what have I got to lose? Do I really want to hang onto this fog that has enveloped my whole life?*

Writing this letter felt safe.

Coming out of the reverie, I felt safe, and

continued writing.

I wanted to tell Wendy everything.

Alarm bells that only I could hear began clanging in my head. Immediately the carefully selected script sprang into life.

"Yes, I'm relieved he's gone. He suffered in the end. We all did, watching him fade away."

With that, the die was cast: this was the politically correct thing to say, and I was playing the game of manicuring the truth, the game I'd learned so well to play. You were a good teacher, Mum.

Turning over the page of the pad, I continued writing, the words flowing easily from the gel-tip pen onto the page.

For years I observed the family and discovered that everyone has secrets. Everyone had much to protect, many hidden agendas. And they had a hidden agenda about me. They had their own ideas about how I should feel, what I should say, what I should do... and I don't give a shit about what they think I should feel, think, say, or do.

The Family — *La Famiglia* — I hated seeing it this way, that image of Sicilians set in concrete by the movie *The Godfather*. I knew our family had not been involved in any way with the Mafia, yet there was so much about the Mafia way of life that permeated our family life, Mum. The code of silence which can't be broken under any circumstances; the double standards — do what we say, don't do what we do; the use of force or threat as the way of settling every conflict, difference of opinion or clash of ideas; veneration of elders; and of course, the big one, honour.

Even now, in my fifties, I was still struggling to get that stuff out of my head! Why did I keep wondering, weighing up, considering everyone else's points of view? Why did I keep giving them power?

Why didn't I just get on with what I wanted to do?

The invisible chains still chafed, tethering me to a way of life and being that was not of my choosing.

I didn't have to play games with Wendy or sanitise the truth. Yet, I couldn't escape the morass of guilt and shame that sucked me into its vortex, like quicksand, when I tried to shake it off.

There are only two emotions I remember feeling as I was growing up — shame and rage.

The shame of what had been happening in our family for so many years. The shame about him, about myself, about the antiquated beliefs and rituals in our family that seemed to have no place in the world today. Shame was an uninvited guest that had drifted in...and stayed.

I was in my teens when *The Godfather* was released. I hated that movie, yet I couldn't turn away from watching it. I was intrigued to see that I had been raised the same as other Sicilians in other parts of the world. That was an eye-opener for me. I remember comparing my own experience with the story unfolding on the screen.

How comforting it was to know that it wasn't just our family that put on big, over-the-top weddings, christenings and confirmations, where respect for elders bordered on elder worship, courtship practices were downright medieval, and food was central to family life.

You never knew, though, how I cringed and blushed with shame in the darkened cinema to see the characters resolve their differences and get their own way with force and threats; how saying one thing and meaning another sometimes meant the difference between life and death; how young children were raised without boundaries and without learning to control their frustrations and disappointments. And how male children grew up to behave like the angry demi-gods of Greek mythology.

And of course, my outrage at how men treated women.

I knew that Sicilians in *my* home country of

Australia were tarred with the same brush as that Mafia family in the U.S., simply because they originated from the same place.

Where are you from? I was often asked when I was growing up.

I always replied, *I was born here, in Australia.*

But what's your background? they continued.

Italian, I would say, *my parents are from Italy, and I was born here.*

I never said Sicilian, at least not at first. I gagged on the word. My gut would turn, and I'd feel sick.

What part of Italy? they persisted.

Even before the words formed in my head, shame turned up, its invisible hands gripping my throat like a vice.

The south, Sicily, rasped my throat, speaking the words I dared not say out loud.

And then it would come, as I always knew it would.

Oh, Mafia...

The one comment that always managed to transform the ripple into a tsunami. My ethnicity was exposed and found wanting. In their eyes, I'd never be able to come back from that.

Rising from deep inside me, seizing my stomach, and turning my face bright crimson, shame engulfed me. I was never able to ride this wave. I was always swallowed up, tossed about like a ragdoll in a hurricane.

And then my defences would spring into action. Like an army of antibodies, I'd defend the country, the culture, you, my parents, my family, myself, often by pointing out their ignorance about the country and its history.

"Your knowledge of Sicily comes from populist movies like The Godfather and stories you've heard or read about in the papers," I would tell them with rising nationalistic fervour.

The irony was lost on such people. In a country populated by convicts and ex-cons, their descendants now took the moral high ground and passed judgement on others.

People who live in glass houses...

Now, when Australians find a bushranger in their ancestry, they wear that as a badge of honour.

Even better, getting married in a "quaint" old Sicilian village overlooking the Mediterranean Sea is now, in the twenty-first century, the height of chic!

I used to tell myself that they were no better. Two hundred years might separate them from their origins, but their origins remained convict, even with all their airs and graces. At least Sicilians entered Australia as free people.

Australians take themselves a lot less seriously these days. They tell jokes, like the one where a Scotsman on entering Australia is asked by the Border Force official whether he has a criminal record. Without missing a beat, he replies, *"Do I need one to get into Australia?"*

I too make light of it now. With a wink and a smile, I mock the threat contained in the most famous line from the movie: *"I might have to make you an offer you can't refuse."*

For most Sicilians, though, a criminal record is a very serious matter, a matter of honour.

I turned to a new page of the writing pad and took a moment to adjust my eyes, blinking a few times. The room around me snapped back into view, as though I'd just come out of a tunnel. I read over what I'd just written and realised I had taken an unexpected detour following one of the many threads of my story.

"Was he ill for some time, or was it sudden and unexpected?" Wendy asked, attempting to recover from her awkward reaction.

I didn't have to play games with Wendy, but I put on my best matter-of-fact voice, like a corporate voice recording: 'Press 1 for PC (politically correct); Press 2 for uncomfortable truth; Press 3 for bullshit.'

"Yes, he'd been ill for some time, so it wasn't unexpected. He suffered at the end, as we all did, watching him," I said, knowing she would think of me as the concerned loving daughter.

I told it as it was.

It **was** awful watching the life ebb out of him day by day. It was pathetic watching you too, holding onto him with an ever-tightening grip.

You couldn't let him go, but he wanted to go.

Why you wouldn't or couldn't let him go was beyond me, after all you'd been through with him. Deep inside, in my most private thoughts, I wished he would go sooner rather than later.

Sitting in that hospital room, watching his laboured breathing as he slept, I asked him silently inside my head, *What are you hanging on for? What are you waiting for? Not only did you have everyone running after you at your beck and call in life, now in death, you're doing the same. Your own needs come before everyone else's — again. Die, won't you...*

"When is the funeral?" asked Wendy, her voice bringing me back to the present, back to the phone.

"It's on New Year's Eve," I replied, "so, look, thanks for the invitation to your New Year's Eve party, but I don't think I'll be in any frame of mind to come along."

"Sure, I understand, but if you change your mind, you're welcome to come." There was a finality in Wendy's tone that told me the conversation was at an end, and I was glad of it.

Playing games wears me out. That's the truth.

I don't have to play games with you now any more either.

The truth is, I was glad he was dead.

For hours afterwards, I ruminated about that phone call, the invitation, the opportunity to celebrate.

Did I want to miss out on an opportunity to celebrate? What would I celebrate?

His life?

No – I wanted to celebrate his death.

A smile began to creep over my face. The idea was tantalising, and it fit with my view of myself as a rule-breaker, a rebel.

A NYE party would be the wake I knew you wouldn't hold.

Sicilians don't have wakes, do you, Mum? Sicilians have morbid get-togethers, where everyone is dressed in funereal clothes, and no one quite knows what to say to console the grieving family. So, they fill the awkward gaps with weak throwaway lines that feign concern for the widow.

There are rules about everything, so everyone attending the funeral is expected to wear black as a mark of grief. Colour, even the slightest hint, is prohibited. Do you remember when I wanted to wear black and white when your father passed away and you ruled it out?

"You can't wear colour to a funeral, it is disrespectful. What will people say?" you fussed.

It served as a reminder to wear what I was expected to wear to Dad's funeral. I had a choice to make: play along and do what is expected, or do what I wanted.

In the end, I decided that Dad's funeral was not

the time or place to put revolution on display and 'come out' as an independent thinker. That would have meant being a rebel, and non-conformity was a threat. It would have been viewed with shock and horror, and invited infamy and insult from others attending the funeral. I knew it was all part of the show—Sicilians love their melodrama. I decided not to play into their hands and give them more to gossip about.

I came to pity him in the end. He had become frail and weak, and his hair had turned grey many years earlier. His skin had also turned grey and paper-thin, giving the impression that it might flake if touched. Every vein protruded from the surface of his hands, like rivers of molten lava pouring down the sides of Mt Etna, his birthplace. He had lost the spare tyre around his middle, which had been a permanent fixture for over forty years. Was this the man who had been the cause of so much fear and anxiety for most of my life? It was hard to imagine now, as I watched him motionless on the bed.

In the end, he was a mere specter of the person he had once been.

When I asked you if you wanted to hold a wake after the funeral, it was as much to find out what you wanted as to know the culturally appropriate thing to do.

"No," you said. You didn't want anyone coming to your place for a wake after the funeral. You just wanted to go home, close the doors and draw the curtains.

Great, I thought. *I don't have to hang around after the funeral.*

At some point during the funeral preparations, I decided to hold a wake of my own.

Hell, what would *la famiglia* say if they knew I was going to a NYE party after attending my own father's funeral? It wouldn't go down well. There would be a lot of talk and gossip about me.

To hell with it, I thought.

The funeral was held mid-morning on New Year's Eve in 35°C heat and sixty per cent humidity. In such uncomfortably sticky weather, I put on the black dress I had bought for the occasion, black stockings and shoes, and prepared my black handbag. Wearing dark sunglasses, black hat, and red lipstick, I went to Dad's funeral.

I went along with the game of keeping up appearances.

After such a day, I was ready for a change of mood. I ended up not going to Wendy's NYE party. I went to the biggest NYE party in town, with my husband, George, on the riverbank.

I drank Champagne, watched the fireworks, and laughed at the stupid things people did when they'd had too much to drink, all under the cover of the anonymity I craved. I was lifted, supported, and carried along by the tide of the crowd's euphoria that erupted at the stroke of midnight.

Good riddance, I said silently to myself, as I raised my glass to toast the dawning of the New Year.

What pleasure it gave me to know that he was

finally gone.

Actually, it wasn't so much pleasure as an indescribable emptiness. I drank to escape the numbness gnawing away at my insides. I hoped the alcohol would make me feel something, anything.

Feeling wasted was better than feeling empty.

Feeling empty was better than feeling scorn.

I told myself that this would be a new beginning.

I was celebrating freedom, feeling free from some invisible burden.

So why did I still feel empty and numb?

I lifted the pen off the page and began to reflect on this man I had identified throughout my life as my father, but whom I had never known at all.

What did I have to fear from this man?

What did any of us have to fear from this man, this man who had brought us little else but misery and fear, a man who with one twitch of his eyebrow, or *that* look, could get us to do whatever he wanted. You didn't cross this man; you didn't stand up to him either. You couldn't have a conversation with him or a discussion of any sort. He always wanted to win the argument and he didn't care how he won it, whether with arguments (rarely), or with lies (often), or with insults and slurs against your character (mostly).

He was a slithering, slimy snake and I am not sorry he's dead!

Even as I watched him lying lifeless in the hospital bed, even then I couldn't let myself acknowledge that thought. I told myself that I was relieved he was dead because he had suffered a great deal, and it was a relief for him and the family. His suffering was finally over.

I was deluding myself, playing games of smoke and mirrors, into believing that I was a dutiful daughter and that was how a dutiful daughter should feel.

I have to be honest with you, Mum. I can't go on playing the game you taught me so well, the game of doing what everyone expects of you, and keep smiling.

I haven't shed any tears for him, either when he died, or in the years since his death.

Maybe the tears will come some time... and maybe they won't.

Now that's something a dutiful daughter wouldn't do—never shed tears for her father!

At the time, I believed I hadn't wept for him in order to be strong for you. Yep, it was my job to support you and be strong for you... how it has always been. Always plastering over my own pain, fear, anxiety, so I could support you. You had always come before me, before anything else in my life.

And just when I thought you would be as relieved as I was to see him gone, you became a blubbering mess. You were usually the strong one, the one who could take just about anything.

But not this time.

After the decades of abuse you endured at the hands of this man, I was shocked that you were shedding any tears for him at all.

Were these tears for him, or for you?

For some people, having a toxic relationship with a partner is better than having no relationship at all. Was that what your tears were about? The loss of your toxic partner, being left alone, after so many years of defining yourself not by who you were but by who you were not? Were you frightened that you didn't know who you were and what you could do any more?

If they were just tears of grief, I could understand that. But what really astounded me after he died were the accusations, the recriminations, not against him but against me!

You accused me of not being there when he died.

You blamed me for not doing enough for him, and for you, when he was in hospital in the weeks before he died.

You accused me of not coming often enough to spend time with him and you. You were there at his bedside every day and every night, towards the end, like the dutiful wife you were.

You saved your most withering attacks for me. I should have been there on Christmas Day and brought him something to eat... while he was in a coma.

You were beyond irrational.

Inconsolable and alone for the first time in your life, you needed a scapegoat.

As usual, I was handy.

It was always someone else's fault.

I thought I understood you. I thought you would have been as glad to see him gone as I was. I thought you would have been relieved to be free of your abuser, your gaoler, your jealousy-crazed husband.

I put my pen down and, for what seemed the longest time, looked at the words I had just written.

I realised I was picking a scab off an old wound that had never healed, and soon, I knew, 'stuff' would come bubbling to the surface.

The act of writing this letter was breaking Sicilians' strictest rule: *omertà* — silence.

Complying with that rule had brought me nothing but misery. I had always been a rule-breaker, or at least a rule challenger, as you know, Mum. That was why you branded me a 'rebel'.

I wore, and still wear, that label as a badge of honour!

Encouraged by this thought, a smile crept over my face. I picked up the pen again and took out another sheet of paper.

Chapter 2

How does it feel to be in prison, Mum? The words glided onto the new page through the gel tip of my pen.

The warm golden glow in the room from the leadlight lamp on my desk, the peace in the house, the silence in the world outside - a stark contrast to my churning inner turmoil.

What do you mean? I imagined you asking.

How did it feel to be in prison, not for something you'd done, but for something you hadn't done?

If you'd done something wrong and got a gaol term for it, the sentence would be justifiable. Prison time comes to an end after a certain period, and in most cases, you get another chance back in society.

But what if you were in prison for something you *hadn't* done? A prison that had no walls, or ceiling, or floor?

What if it was inside you, carried with you by you every day, in your head.

Except you didn't even realise that you were.

Let's say you were in prison, not for looking at another man, but for the *possibility* that you *might* look at another man. You married a stranger and after two years apart, he took you, a beautiful young woman of twenty-four, into a boarding house full of single young men, and if you so much as glanced at one of them, even in passing in the corridor, he beat you up, imagining that you'd been unfaithful.

In time you learned to avoid passing these men in the dark narrow corridors of the old weatherboard Queenslander that served as a boarding house. You learned to avoid showering in the unisex showers when they were around. But there was always someone around. You learned that despite your protestations, your husband never stopped beating you because, in his mind, you had been unfaithful.

Let's look at other things you didn't do but that you were serving time for. You were in prison for not cooking the meals he wanted to eat, every day, even though you had no idea what they were. And of course, he didn't tell you.

Remember those times when you went out of your way to try cooking new things just to please him? Dad had just finished building that house in Spring Hill, so there were new appliances in the kitchen, a beautiful large stove and oven, a luxury at that time, fresh paint on the newly plastered walls and corniced ceilings, tastefully selected tiles on the floor, and a balcony with a view out to the city when City Hall was still the tallest building in Brisbane. The SGIO building was under construction and would be taller than City Hall in time.

Because he worked in construction, he knocked off at four each afternoon and was home by about five. He'd sit at the kitchen table with you, glass of beer in hand, and tell you something about his day. In the hotter months, he reeked of sweat mixed with dirt and cement covering his clothes and boots, face and hands.

After downing a cold beer, he would have a shower and expect dinner on the table by 6.00 pm, eaten in the company of the nightly news on television, and the family.

It was a routine that took place every day with stifling regularity. Even on Saturdays and Sundays. He worked six, sometimes seven days a week, just to get ahead. In later years, I heard from several people that Italians were hard workers who acquired everything through hard work and the sweat of their brow. In my later years, I found it gratifying to hear that Australians recognised that characteristic of Sicilians and didn't attribute their successes to involvement with the Mafia or a generous godfather, as so many had in the 1960s.

What took place, also with discomforting regularity at that time, were his eruptions.

Do you know what I found particularly terrifying?

How he exploded, suddenly and unexpectedly, and not knowing what triggered his outbursts.

I was all of eight when I became aware of this. Dad came out of the shower, ready to sit down to eat a home-cooked meal after a hard day's work, and then he erupted with no forewarning.

It never crossed my mind at that time why you were trying out different dishes, until you told me many years later.

It had started early in your marriage. He didn't like the food you prepared, and instead of telling you what he liked, or how he preferred it to be cooked, he yelled abuse at you while hurling his plate of food out the window or against the kitchen walls. In his mind, you were deliberately preparing meals he did not enjoy, even though he was earning the money by the sweat of his brow. In his view, he was justified in punishing such deliberate acts of persecution.

He would then storm out of the house, leaving you in tears.

When he returned hours later, he would demand, "Have you made me something else to eat? What do you do all day? Why can't you make me something I like, like my mother used to make?"

Frightened, you'd reply that you hadn't prepared anything else because you didn't know what he liked to eat.

After all this fuss, he ordered you to make him poached eggs.

But before he took his first mouthful, he insisted that you taste and swallow the first bite, in his presence, just in case. In his suspicious mind, you were capable of lacing his food with the rat poison that everyone commonly had in their homes at that time.

This continued for many years.

Being his food-taster was the *antipasto* for what was to come. You could never have imagined that your marriage would get off to such a bizarre start.

He'd stomp out of the house after his fits of rage. I never knew where he went. When he returned home, he was usually jovial, as if nothing had happened. He never gave a second thought to how he had left his wife and young children. But I saw the pain and hurt his actions caused us all.

Hurling his plate outside was the way you found out what he liked and what he didn't like.

Sometimes, the plates landed in the back yard of our Calabrian neighbours. There was no love lost between Sicilians and Calabrese, and they often hurled insults at one another in a game of one-upmanship. It seemed deadly serious to me when I was eight or nine years old.

Our Calabrese neighbours were a family of mum, dad, and a daughter named Bianca, and we never spoke to that family.

Mother was short and round. She wore black-rimmed glasses and a permanent scowl. I never once saw her smile. What she lacked in height she more than made up for with her voice.

Father was a henpecked doormat who suffered

his wife's soul-crushing nagging in silence. I often heard her screeching her daughter's name, "Biaaaaanca!" , or if she was in a bad mood, and it seemed like she was always in a bad mood, the call was short and clipped.

I often saw four-year-old Bianca look longingly over the fence at us, hoping to join us in play.

That never happened though—I guess Mother thought we might contaminate her daughter with Sicilian germs.

Their back yard was a dump. The rotting timber fence marking the boundary between their property and ours was on its last legs, the grass was waist-deep for an adult, and scattered throughout the long grass were rusty trellises, paint-splattered ladders, splotchy timber planks of various lengths, empty rusting paint tins, and garbage needing to be burned in the backyard incinerator.

And one day, there was a baby goat in the grass, not more than a few weeks old.

As an eight-year-old, I imagined that the goat

was a pet for Bianca. She didn't seem to have anyone else to play with, and she seemed to enjoy playing with it. I looked over the fence often, hoping to be allowed to go over there and pat the dear sweet thing.

One evening, Dad hurled his plate of food out the window landing in their back yard.

Next morning at six, the shrew called out, "Eh, *puttana Siciliana* (trans. Sicilian whore), your plate's here. My goat ate the food, but your plate's here in shards. Your husband missed my goat by inches. If he hits my goat next time, you'll see what happens... So, your husband doesn't like your cooking, eh?" she cackled vindictively. When she ran out of breath, she took a deep breath and roared again.

Such mocking, especially from a Calabrese, just added insult to injury for you.

One day, the goat vanished. When I told you, without looking up from shelling peas, you replied, "They've probably eaten it."

That did my head in. I was horrified. I had become

attached to that kid, watching it hop playfully around in the back yard, its pristine white coat clearly visible in amongst the tall grass. I just could not make sense of how anyone could kill and eat such an innocent young thing.

Then one day, we moved, and I never saw those people again. I never saw that henpecked, silently seething man, his shrill shrew of a wife, nor the little girl with the big round sad eyes looking longingly over the fence at what might have been.

And Dad stopped hurling his dinner out the window at the new place.

He was in his early forties by that time, I'm guessing. His black hair had started to thin out and go grey at the temples, and his waist was thickening. The hard work he did each day did not seem to keep him slim.

Once home, he never wanted to do anything, and in fact, he left many jobs around the house unfinished. We had just the one car, a Holden sedan the colour of mint green, that served both for family and for work. There was also only the one driver in the family. During the work week the vehicle was filled with tools, dusty bags of cement, rags, and any other paraphernalia Dad needed in his line of work. Then on Sundays it was up to me, as the eldest, to wash and spit-polish it for family outings.

At various times he played games with us and expected to win every time. He loved playing draughts against his children, and, while we were young, he always won. As we got older, we refused to play with him. In doing so, we deprived him of the pleasure of winning. We also avoided being on the receiving end of his displeasure when he lost. He revelled in winning, like a child who had never won a thing in his life. It made him so happy to win against his own children. It never seemed to occur to him that he could teach us how to win at the game.

He also played a game of speed, 'hot hands' or 'slapsies', with all of us kids. You remember how it went.

He used to place his hand, palm down, on the table, and, pretending to be slow, he allowed us to slap his hand. The goal of the game was for the slapper to hit the back of his hand before he, the slappee, could pull his hand away. Because the slappee's goal was to pull their hand away, the slapper had to act quickly and deftly. Getting a 'hit' was a win that permitted the slapper to have another go.

In this game, he would allow us to slap his hand a few times, to lull us into believing that we had outsmarted him. This was the only time we were allowed to hit our father, so we were always very tentative and cautious.

Once we were pacified into a false sense of security, he pulled his hand away swiftly and suddenly, leaving us confused and horrified. When we missed his hand and slammed the table instead, the players swapped roles and the game continued. The child, now the slappee, put her hand on the table and it was his turn to slap. With this 'winning' strategy, he always triumphed over his children.

When I played this game with him as a child, what I remember most is the feeling of joyful optimism I entertained as I fancied that I could maybe win. It was always mixed with a sense of foreboding that was never far away though. Over time, that sense of dread grew, overshadowing any bright-eyed optimism I might still have harboured, as I learned that the game always turned out the same way.

He played this game like it was a gunfight.

He played with us as if we were his 'playthings'.

The odds were stacked heavily against me, against any child, daring to test themselves against him. He seemed to take some kind of sadistic pleasure in keeping us suspended in uncertainty however long he liked, as he watched his child-opponent squirm and fidget with rising anticipation and anxiety.

There was only one way this 'game' turned out... ever.

Looking intently into his eyes — maybe I thought they would betray his intentions in the next millisecond — I placed my hand gingerly on the table, all the while his eyes stared unflinchingly into mine. Then he held his hand over mine, the gunfighter readying himself for the 'hit'.

The longer his hand hovered over mine on the table, the more anxious I became, as I waited for the blow. My eyes darted up and down between his face and his hand, trying to spot the slightest flicker of a finger or twitch of an eye that might suggest he was ready to pounce. Being on the defence I would pull my hand away again and again to avoid the inevitable.

Then it happened. Like a bolt of lightning, expected yet unexpectedly, his hand smashed down onto mine, crushing my hand... and more.

I'll never forget his maniacal grin, the deep-bellied guffaw, and his face flushed red from the climactic excitement of the win. He used to laugh at my impotence and lack of speed and strategy, his taunts hurting more than any physical slap. Then he'd lecture me on how to beat him: be faster next time.

42

Physically, the effect of these 'games' was temporary: a tear-streaked face, a racing heart, a red-hot hand. What you never saw, though, is the longer lasting impact of the game. Smarting from his rebukes, and ashamed of being defectively small and impotent, I always ended up feeling crumpled.

I had only one choice—not to play. That was a hard lesson, learned painfully over time when the dread of humiliation became greater than the fantasy that I might win. Disillusioned at a young age, yet determined not to drown in shame, I decided not to play his power games any more.

Watching him play this game with my younger siblings, I learned that it was about power for him—making us understand that he was bigger, stronger, and more powerful than us, always, in all ways. As a young girl, what happened in these games just reinforced him in my eyes as our *Padre Padrone*, Father and Master.

Do you remember when this all came back to

haunt him years later?

It was when my own children were under ten.

You would both come to visit of an evening just when we were having dinner. One evening when George was away, the old man started this game with my seven-year-old, Remy. You might remember, he was a tiny slip of a child at that time. Dad was enjoying himself immensely playing 'slapsies' with my son, but my little boy was not.

Time seemed to stand still. Dad glared at Remy, a tomcat watching his prey intently. My son was skittish, looking up at his grandfather, then looking down at his bright red hand, and then back up again. Up, down, up, down, his eyes flashed, trying to predict when his grandfather would strike, trying to outwit and out-pace the old man, all the while darting his hand back and forth on the table to avoid the inevitable strike on his stinging hand. A sense of déjà vu came over me.

He was just seven, no match for a much older and wilier opponent.

Remy's angry red hand was becoming increasingly a reflection of the growing fear, frustration, and humiliation inside him.

"Dad, stop, you're hurting him," I pleaded.

He continued, riveted to the game.

"Paolo, *fermeti* (stop). You're hurting the child," you pleaded.

That surprised me, since I don't remember you ever telling him to stop hurting us.

So focused was he on the 'game' that he appeared not to hear. He just kept 'playing' and slapping my son's little hand harder and harder, chortling each time he got a 'hit'. Remy was close to tears, but he kept putting his hand down on the table, and he kept getting whacked.

Then, out of left field, nine-year-old Albert gave Dad a hard push, sending this barrel-shaped sixty-six-year-old man hurtling onto the polished ironwood floor with his legs in the air, the chair between his legs. I was shocked, but glad that the torture of my little boy was over. Suddenly though, I had a horrible sick feeling in the pit of my stomach, dreading what might happen next. Experience told me to expect an eruption.

I rushed forward to help him up, suppressing the urge to laugh because he looked like a beetle on his back, arms and legs flailing in the air, grasping for some invisible lifeline to hold onto.

A mixture of shock, dread, *schadenfreude*, a need to laugh to relieve the tension... The emotions just came rolling over me, like mists from the ocean, enveloping me, fogging my brain so I couldn't see clearly any more what I needed to do.

Slowly he picked himself up off the floor, shook my hand off him, as though my attempts at helping him emphasised his weakness, and limped towards the front door.

Without turning, he called out to you, as if talking to a dog, "Are you coming?"

Silently, you picked up your bag and jacket and followed him out to the car. I saw the look of fear in your eyes. Without a word, I followed you to the front door, and saw you out.

I watched your car drive away until it rounded the corner and I could no longer see the tail-lights.

I dreaded what would happen on the way back home, and once you arrived home.

I decided I couldn't worry about that—he had brought it upon himself. He should have stopped much earlier.

He should have stopped when he saw the pain on his grandson's face.

Truth is, he just didn't know when to stop. His own pleasure was more important to him than his grandson's pain. He seemed to have no feeling at all for the child and might not even have realised that his actions were hurting my son.

As I turned to come back into the living room, I knew that my children would be shell-shocked.

With my heart still pounding in my chest, I returned to the scene and saw Albert, his eyes open wide, like a deer in headlights. Remy was nursing his red-hot hand, at a loss as to what to do or where to look. The younger ones were also shocked into silence. Four children under ten with nothing to say... now that was a first!

I walked back into the living room, still trembling, looked at them, and said, "Well, that stopped him, didn't it?" letting out a nervous little laugh, trying to lighten the situation. No matter what happened next, these children were more important to me than the old man. More important to me than life itself.

Why was I trembling, you might ask. That scene took me right back to scenes I had witnessed when I was around Albert's age, and older. I too had been traumatised by what I had seen and experienced. Those scenes came flashing back and the fear was there in my body exactly as it had been all those years ago, as if no time had elapsed. I had been waiting for the explosion that night, but it never came. Sometimes no eruption was worse than the explosion itself.

Not wanting my children to be traumatised, I

instinctively gathered them together. When I put my arms out to envelop them, Albert recoiled, thinking I was going to smack him for hurting *Nonno*, Grandfather.

"I'm not going to hurt you, Albert. You've done nothing wrong," I reassured him.

"Actually, Nonno had it coming." I could see that Albert was bewildered.

"Nonno should have known better," I told him and his siblings.

"He is the adult. He should have stopped a lot earlier without being told."

"I didn't intend to hurt Nonno," Albert blurted. "I just wanted him to stop hurting Rem."

What could I do, Mum?

That was one of those moments when I felt time slow down, when the weight of the past came crashing up against what I knew would be best for them in the future.

Should I do things the way they'd always been done, according to tradition, or should I go the way I believed they should be done now? Follow tradition, or follow my gut instinct about what was right for them. Tradition demanded that I punish my nine-year-old son severely for hurting not only an older person, but his grandfather at that. Tradition considered my son to be at fault.

I made my decision, and immediately felt the conviction flow through me like life-giving energy.

I put my arm around Albert.

"You did a very brave thing here tonight, rescuing your little brother," I reassured him.

I sat down on the couch with my boys and wrapped my arms around them.

"I don't blame you for what's happened this evening," I continued. "I don't think that Nonno will be playing that game again anytime soon."

I spoke to them calmly, soothing me as well as them.

In the days following that incident, you told your sister, Orazia, about what had happened that evening.

"Francesca's children are at fault," she judged. "They were badly behaved, hurting their grandfather like that. And Francesca is at fault for not raising her children right, like us."

Childless herself, she was one of those armchair experts who sanctimoniously passed judgement on others.

I had no time for such people.

Do you know what it felt like to be constantly in a tug-of-war with myself, one side saying, 'Follow tradition, do things the way they've always been done', the other side saying, 'do what you know is right', when you knew that what was right was often diametrically opposed to the way they'd always been done in your traditional Sicilian culture?

I felt the chafing of uncompromising chains binding me to tradition, yet I knew there was safety in following the same traditions that everybody adhered to. By taking the traditional approach, I was sure not to attract the reproach of your mother and sisters, the self-proclaimed torchbearers of tradition.

But as a mother, my children always won out.

I was on a collision path with the traditionalists... and I loved it!

As the days and weeks ticked over, it was clear that an impasse had developed. You and Dad didn't come to visit any more, and the kids grew more and more nervous about that. They thought that Nonno was holding a grudge. Maybe he was. Or maybe 'Goliath' couldn't face the nine-year-old giant-slayer! It became clear that I had to do something to break the impasse.

I knew Dad wouldn't apologise for hurting Remy. Sicilian men don't apologise. They're always right, aren't they, even when they're not. I knew I would have to make the first move.

One day, a few weeks after that night, I took Albert aside.

"I would like you to apologise to your grandfather for hurting him, Albert," I told him.

"But he was hurting Rem," he replied, an edge of

fear in his voice.

"That's true, we both know that. But Nonno will never apologise for hurting your brother."

I could see that he was scared.

"You said it yourself, you didn't intend to hurt him. That's what you'll say. And I'll be right there beside you. I will not leave you to face Nonno alone."

Albert reluctantly agreed.

The next time we visited, I approached Dad with Albert, who apologised to his grandfather, saying that he had not intended to hurt him. He was pale with fear, and the apology stammered from his lips.

Putting his arm around Albert's shoulders, Dad reassured him it was all good. I knew then that it was over, that peace had come between the old man and the young.

Many years later, these events sometimes still find their way into my thoughts. I reflect on how difficult it was for Dad to control himself, his passions, his frustrations, his actions, and how impossible it was for him to say sorry. To my knowledge, he never once apologised for anything. But when he led my son away with a benevolent smile, I knew that was his version of an apology.

Dad never played 'slapsies' again with my children or with any of his other grandchildren. He had learned his lesson, taught by a nine-year-old who was protecting his little brother. I believe that Dad saw it like that. Maybe he also felt some sadness because none of his own older brothers had ever done anything like that to protect or rescue him when he was growing up. I think he came out of that time with a newfound respect for my nine-year-old. Years later, when I reflected on those events, I realised that the man who was my father was still a boy, and that the boy, my nine-year-old son, became a man that day.

Dad always wanted to win, no matter what, no matter who he hurt or steamrolled in the process, as long as he got what he wanted. Even when he was half dead.

Do you remember the first time he told you he loved you?

It was in hospital, on his deathbed.

You had been with him the whole time he was in hospital. You barely went home, usually just for a change of clothes and to prepare one of his favourite dishes to bring back to him. You were exhausted yourself, while he was looked after and kept comfortably medicated. He never got out of bed in his last days, and he was unconscious most of the time. Eating was optional for him, yet if he craved a beer, he had one.

You told me how one morning, early, after you'd spent the previous night in an armchair by his side, he awoke and saw you, dishevelled, and became aware that you had been there all night. Realising that he would never return alive to the home he had built for you both only a few years earlier, he began to open up to you in ways he never had before. Despite the morphine coursing through his veins, this was a rare moment of clarity during his last days.

He opened up by telling you that he loved you, that he had always loved you, from the first time he had seen you back home.

Weary from the prolonged vigil and sensing no longer the need for the protective armour you always wore around him, you laughed it off, replying that it was a bit late for declarations of love, telling him that he should have said it years ago, in loving ways rather than through violence.

That was the first time he had said that he loved you, in a marriage that had lasted more than four decades.

I imagine he felt humiliated by the rebuke.

In his weakened state, he lifted his arm slowly, hand balled into a fist, and brought his arm down to strike you across the face. Fortunately, you saw the blow coming, unlike all the others during your marriage. You retreated to avoid it, then kept your distance from his bedside. You weren't a young woman either by then, but you were still agile enough to avoid being hurt any more.

In telling you he loved you, he had made himself vulnerable for the first, and last, time. He slipped away into a coma after that, never having expressed remorse, never apologising for anything.

He died as he had lived — still trying to prove he was a man.

Chapter 3

Maletto, Sicily

They married in January 1952 in the small town of Maletto, nearly a thousand metres above sea level. The cold wind sent light snow eddies swirling around members of the wedding party and guests, sprinkling them with snow-flakes, as they stood on the Via Matrice entrance to the *Chiesa Madre SS Cuori di Gesù e Maria* which opened out onto a wide stairway leading down to the *piazza*.

Billowing in the wind, the bride's customary white dress was made of thin cotton which provided no protec-tion against the bone-aching cold. After the war, that was all her parents could afford. He was twenty-six, she was twenty-one.

I stopped writing, raised the pen from the sheet, and realised what I was doing... again.

I was trying to understand you, understand the world through your eyes. I'd made a habit of it over the years and it had served me well. If I could understand you, I reasoned, I would be able to predict what you would say and do and protect myself against your attacks by thinking up responses to the sometimes-crazy things you said. I was going to be ready, I told myself.

Maybe I could even break free, if I was lucky...

It didn't always work though.

Like prey getting to know its predator, I watched, waited, listened, learned, found an opportunity... and made a run for it, only to get caught... again and again.

One day I'll be free, I told myself over and over.

One day...

How many times did I think this? How many times did the thought of freedom keep me going when there was nothing else to support or encourage me?

This thought faded away like the last note of a reverie I sometimes played on my upright piano.

I began sifting through the stories you told me over many years about Maletto.

Your courtship was short, just a couple of months, typical of that time.

Dad had expressed interest in courting you when he saw you crossing the *piazza* on more than one occasion. His desire to court you was conveyed to your father through the local matchmaker, as custom dictated.

On official commencement of the courtship, couples like you and Dad were never permitted to be alone together. One evening, Dad invited you to the cinema with him. According to custom, your whole family went along to chaperone you. Paolo sat at one end of the row, while you sat at the other end... and in between there was your father, mother, and your five brothers and sisters. Males are the hunter, and females, the hunted, according to the elders. The hunter was encouraged to go out and sow his wild oats before marriage. However, when the time came to select a woman for marriage, the female had to be perfect, untouched and unblemished.

This belief was even cemented in your folklore: 'There are women to play with and women to marry'.

In one unguarded moment when you were alone with him, Paolo planted a kiss on your cheek.

You rebuked him, telling him not to do that again.

He tried again some weeks later. This time, he kissed you on the lips. You pulled away from him and told him that if he tried it again, you would send him away.

His reply?

"I had to try that," he said. "I wanted to see if you allowed me to kiss you. If you had, I would have broken up with you then and there. It would have told me that you liked it. And then I would have wondered how many other men you had allowed to kiss you."

That would have meant that you were cheap and easy, and therefore dishonourable.

Whatever defiled a woman's honour defiled the honour of the men in her life, whether they were her father, brothers, or husband. In Sicily in the early 1950s, a simple kiss planted on a virgin's lips was enough to defile a woman's honour.

It took me a long time to get my head around this idea of honour and dishonour, Mum. You grew up immersed in this culture, in this way of thinking, so for you, it made sense. You and I often argued about it over the years I was growing up, and I would point to the gaping holes in that way of thinking, but you always replied fatalistically: "That's the way it has always been, that's how it will always be. *Che serà serà.*"

It reminded me of the scene in the movie, *The Godfather*, where Michael Corleone courted a young woman in a Sicilian village where he was hiding out. He walked beside her at arm's length. Following right on their heels was a posse of old women dressed in black, the traditional mourning dress, chatting among themselves.

It needed ten old women to chaperone one young girl, to safeguard her chastity, her honour, and the honour of her family!

I realised that this was still going on here in a different country in a different time.

You thought you had changed. You thought that you were thoroughly modern, living in the big city, going through migration, learning a new language, starting your own business, presenting your children to an education system that saw the world differently from you.

But beneath all that, you hadn't changed at all!

If anything, you were more Sicilian than the Sicilians still in their own country.

They moved on. You didn't.

In Sicily, before the Second World War, feudalism still prevailed. It would continue to exist for another two decades, until the aftermath of war brought democracy to a country that had known nothing but autocratic leaders ruling with absolute power throughout millennia. Power was never shared with the people in this country that had been ruled by various forms of European and Moorish aristocracy, a theocracy that believed it had a divine right to rule, and more recently, by 'benevolent' and not so benevolent dictators.

The feudal system was woven into the fabric of society and entrenched in families. Husbands never shared power with their wives. Women were of lesser value than men; they were their possessions, as were the children. Men were absolute masters.

Sons were raised by their parents to expect to be lord and master of their own households one day. They were raised to hold grand expectations, they could never do any wrong (and if they did, the girls were punished on their behalf, so daughters were the whipping 'boys' for their brothers).

Your two families couldn't have been more different though.

Dad was the youngest in a family of nine sons. He wagged school often, preferring to go to the creek with some of the other local street kids also playing truant, so he had barely three years of schooling.

Dad's father was a *murature* (literally, a wall-builder, or a builder and stonemason) who, seeing that his youngest son had no interest in school, took him to work with him. By the age of ten, he was a labourer for his father, carrying weights too heavy for most ten-year-olds emaciated by little food and hard physical labour.

It was a dog-eat-dog world he lived in, and his older brothers were among the worst offenders. They made fun of this boy who would one day be my father. They mocked him, shamed and humiliated him for being less strong, less competent, a 'lesser man' than they. On one occasion, one of his older brothers even threw a knife at him, missing him by centimetres.

Dad's family lived in town in rented premises, living hand to mouth. Despite having several incomes from the older working sons, the family never owned its own home. His brothers squandered their money, mostly on cigarettes and women – the wrong kind. Not surprisingly, some of his brothers succumbed to venereal disease and died young. I can only guess what Dad learned about managing money in this family.

In this male-dominated household, the family lived by unspoken hierarchical rules: kick those below you; suck up to those above you; each man for himself, trust no one – your own brother could stab you in the back; the government is out to get you; and, you don't have to pay your dues, you can threaten or bribe your way out of them.

They lived according to the belief that father had given life; father could take it away, so children had to obey their father.

On the other hand, your family, Mum, was very different.

You were the second eldest in a family of six children, four girls and two boys. Your father owned rural properties which, in feudalistic Sicily in the early twentieth century, made him one of the landed gentry. Later, in the 1970s, he would be awarded the title of *Cavaliere* by the Italian government, the Australian equivalent of a knighthood.

Your parents owned their own home and had farming properties to support the family. Your parents were responsible with money and trained their children to manage it. Your family lived by and modelled the values of resourcefulness, self-responsibility, initiative, and hard work.

When you married, these differences between your family backgrounds became glaringly obvious.

Dad didn't like losing at anything, and he didn't like losing money or being taken for a fool, which was often only in his own mind. I presume that was because it made him feel small and weak, humiliated and ashamed. So he'd hit out at whoever or whatever it was that had triggered those feelings in him. You copped his anger and frustration in the form of violent abuse because, by being who you were, you made him feel that way.

You had six years of schooling to his three, and you were better at managing money. He resented you for it, yet, at the same time, he trusted you with the money he earned.

He attacked your family because he believed they claimed to be better than everyone else. Your father had properties; his father didn't. In the Sicilian feudal hierarchy, Dad's family of stonemasons was much further down the food chain than landowners.

When I was in my teens, it often bewildered me what the fuss was all about, hearing the snarky remarks he made about your family, and the passion with which you defended it.

Of course, I was too young to understand the depth of emotion that lay behind the insults. But it did make me feel torn between you both. I often felt shredded at the things you said to one another. In my youthful innocence, I often told you to leave him. I didn't understand what that entailed, nor why you didn't leave him.

Dad also believed that landowners, including

the Catholic Church, took advantage of the *murature* who, for much of the time, worked for nothing more than the promise of payment upon completion of a job. When they weren't paid, they did what they had to do to get compensated for their work. Threats were not uncommon, neither was theft. Dad both needed them and hated them at the same time.

He believed that priests abused their power, like so many around him did. He saw that they were well-fed, as they collected a kilo of pasta from this parishioner, half a dozen eggs from that parishioner, or a litre of olive oil from someone else, often for nothing more than speaking the name of a departed loved one during Mass, or offering prayers for a sick family member. Parishioners gave generously of their meagre rations to the Church in return for a measure of spiritual solace.

In response, Dad developed the brash swagger of a tough guy, a *malandrino* (rogue), to intimidate anyone who might even think to cheat him. He would not be taken for a fool.

I have wondered sometimes if he actually ever did nick anything from priests when they failed to pay him.

Those were wild-west times. In the absence of any semblance of social order after the war, people fell back onto the legacy of their inheritance: their code of honour.

Yep, this honour thing was at the root of it all, wasn't it? It was at the root of his beliefs, his expectations, his actions.

It protected him from feeling shame, even if it meant winning games against children.

Was he an honourable man then, my father?

I scribbled the question hastily by the glow of the desk lamp. It was getting late, and George was watching some program alone in the other room.

I sat back in my chair, thinking about the differences between Dad and George.

For me, a man of honour is someone worthy of respect, someone who commands respect yet never demands it, someone who does what he says, who protects the weak and vulnerable, who can be relied upon, someone who is honest and truthful and not always seeking to advantage himself.

I realised I was writing about George.

Was Dad an honourable man?

The funny thing about him was that in some situations he was, but in many others, he was glaringly self-serving.

Remember when you and Dad sponsored your sisters and brothers to come to Australia, to your home, when they first arrived in Australia in the mid-1950s? I recall you telling me of your loneliness in those early years after you arrived here. There was no one to talk to; you couldn't speak English, nor did you go to work. So Dad offered to sponsor your siblings so you wouldn't feel so homesick.

That house we all lived in was a basic low-set

chamfer-board house with paper-thin walls. Your brothers lived in a room under the house built into the side of the hill. As a four or five-year-old, I remember sliding a silver one-shilling coin into the gas meter under the house for hot water and cooking. These meters were right outside their bedroom downstairs.

Your siblings arrived one at a time over a ten-year period. At no time did he take advantage of your unmarried sisters. He understood that he was their chaperone, the one to whom their father had entrusted their welfare, and he was not about to sully his name by taking advantage of them. That made him a man of honour.

It also made him a very generous man. You told me that he accepted no payment whatsoever from your siblings, not rent for the room they occupied, nor even a contribution to the weekly food bill.

But there were also many times I saw him being self-serving, when he lied to get out of something he didn't want to do, or he just put himself and his needs first to the exclusion of everybody else.

Do you remember what he did with the extra shop he built in that little shopping centre that he did not have permission to construct? His attitude was, once it's built, council wouldn't make him demolish it. So he went ahead and built it.

When it was completed, the building inspector came to check on the building for approvals. He informed Dad that it wasn't approved so it could not be used as commercial premises.

"What would he know?" Dad decided, dismissing the inspector with an unceremonious wave of the hand.

He ignored the authorities and leased it out anyway.

When the inspector came around again a few weeks later and found the shop being leased out at commercial rates, Dad was told to shut it down. He was offered an alternative however. If he chose not to shut down the unapproved premises, the whole building would be demolished, and he would be billed for the demolition costs.

Well, that put the fear of God in him, didn't it!

He thought he had outsmarted the council. He must have thought that they were like city officials in Sicily who, on having their palms greased, would give him what he wanted.

Dad thought the city building officials here were fools.

His old-world view came crashing down around his ears when he realised they meant business.

Better the old-world views come crashing down than the building, I guess he decided.

All during this time of construction and the dealings with the council, he did not once listen to you. I was old enough at the time to understand your conversations. You told him that he couldn't just do what he wanted, that the rule of law prevailed here, not like in Sicily, and that he should do things by the book.

He took you for a fool for believing that.

But I was so glad that the council presented him with that ultimatum. It made him aware that the law was greater than he was. In our family though, he was Father and Master; there was no one greater or more powerful than he.

What did he do?

An honourable man would have taken respon-sibility, found out what he needed to do, negotiated a settlement with them, and done what he agreed to do.

What did Dad do instead?

He forced you to sort it all out for him. He didn't like dealing with office people; he was terrified of men in suits and ties. They had power and authority, where he had none in that situation.

He was one of those people who sucked up to those he considered higher up the social ladder than himself, while bullying those he considered below him, like you, his wife. He only respected boundaries that were enforced by legal or physical force. With the men in suits, he backed down very quickly, cowering like a dog with its tail between its legs.

So, you talked to the council inspectors to find out

what was required for the building to be declared legal. You negotiated a solution that you could live with and council could accept. Finally, Dad accepted that solution as well, only because the alternative was destruction of the building and annihilation of his entire investment.

Council had made him an offer he couldn't refuse... in a way he could understand. He had been cornered into 'dropping his pants', where he was used to 'wearing the pants'.

In Sicily where city officials were known to accept bribes, he would have been considered street-smart. But here, in the society of *Inglese*, the English, he had to abide by the law, and the law was the same for all. He wasn't used to that. He thought he could get his own way. He thought he was the law, the judge, jury, and warden.

Talk about notions of grandiosity!

Two months after you were married, he boarded the ship for Australia on a one-way ticket paid for with borrowed money. Like so many others in 1952, he was leaving the old country in search of a new life and fresh opportunities. For two years, he worked on sugar cane farms in north Queensland, like so many other Italians, to pay off his loan and to earn enough money to bring you, his bride, out to join him. Meanwhile, you stayed back in the old country in your father's house until he had saved enough for your one-way ticket.

Chapter 4

He was "hewn from the rock from whence he came: hard, unyielding, unpredictable"

Anonymous

Disembarking from the ship in 1954 in Brisbane, the young woman thought she had landed on another planet. She had believed she was coming to an advanced country. After all, Australia was part of the Allied Forces which had won the war only nine years before.

The passengers picked their way purposefully among the waiting crowd on the wharf. Crammed into the small space, the crowd jostled and scrambled to reunite with loved ones. Despite being squeezed from all sides, the young woman paused momentarily on the wharf to take in her surrounds, her instinctive edginess steadily giving way to shock and horror.

This was not how she had expected the "new world" to look.

Weathered and grey, hardwood timber slats yawned over the expanse of the wharf. Lining the shore, the corrugated iron terminal and warehouses bore an uncanny resemblance to pictures of similar buildings she had seen in books following Italy's annexation and occupation of Abyssinia in 1935.

Making her way slowly through the crowd, searching every face she passed, she tried to find something, someone, familiar to moor her to her new surrounds, her only companion a solitary reinforced cardboard port containing all her worldly possessions.

Weary travellers, glad to finally be on land, reconnected joyfully with waiting friends and families. As they left the wharf, one by one, she was left standing alone, a stranger in a foreign land, an alien language filling her ears. Only the wharfies remained, scuttling back and forth on the dock, unloading cargo.

The young woman made a sad sight.

"Has she come all this way just to be stood up by her fiancé, or worse, her husband?"

The thought was written on their faces as they watched her out of the corner of their eyes.

The young woman grew increasingly agitated. The once crowded dock thinned out over time. Even the wharfies were leaving.

The young woman began wondering what to do. Her husband hadn't turned up to meet her; she didn't know if he had received her letters and telegrams, so she didn't know if he even knew she was arriving that day.

Having never been outside of her parents' home on her own, let alone outside Sicily on her own, she was naïve to the ways of the world. She formulated a plan in her head: if her husband didn't turn up, she would speak with the captain of the ship, tell him her situation, and hope to secure a return berth on the ship back to Italy.

She had just about given up on him when he bounced cheerfully towards her. Taking her brown 1940s' paperboard suitcase, he led her to the waiting car of a friend who had driven him to the wharf.

After two years' separation, and only a small black and white photo of their wedding to remind her, she barely remembered what he looked like.

Relieved, she followed him to the car.

"Did you receive my letters? My telegram?" she asked insistently.

"Si, certo (yes, of course)."

"So you knew I was arriving today?"

"Si."

"Why didn't you let me know that you had received my telegram then? Why didn't you let me know you would be here? Why were you so late in coming?" she pressed through her tears of anxiety mixed with relief.

"I don't write... I took a day off work. I fell asleep and when I woke up, I had to walk to Pippo's place to get him to give me a lift here. Anyway, you should have known I would be here."

"How should I have known that?" she continued interrogating.

Arriving at Pippo's car, the question hung unanswered between them.

That was your introduction to Brisbane, you told me when I was old enough to understand. You just wanted to get back on that ship and return home, you told me.

He didn't have the courtesy to write, to acknowledge your telegram or your letters, you thought. Who is this man that I'm married to? What is this godforsaken place that he has brought me to?

Your first look at Brisbane must have left you feeling marooned, as Pippo drove through city streets. You had grown up in a three-storey stone house with running water inside the house. As you passed street after dusty street, you looked in horror at the old wooden houses with tin roofs, many on stilts, standing on large blocks of land, and realised that they were not sewered... for each house there was an outhouse in the back yard.

And then you arrived at one such place, a men's-only boarding house in inner-city Spring Hill, where he was staying. How thoughtful! From there, you had a view over much of Brisbane where you could see the outhouses all lined up in symmetrical rows and columns. If you could have returned to that ship, I believe you would have.

You hadn't seen each other in two years, and he had not written to you at all, save for the one letter containing your ticket to Australia.

There was no opportunity to get to know each other before you were married either, so you began getting to know each other when you arrived two years later.

By this time, you had your own hopes and dreams of how married life should be, kindled by the tales and homilies your mother and grandmothers had told you:

"Make your husband happy."

"Always smile at him when he comes home from work because you don't know what he's had to put up with during the day."

"You can do whatever you want to do once you're married."

Now that you were married and unchained from the yoke of your father and mother, you thought that you were free to be and do what you wanted.

That was a lie.

It didn't take you long to find out that things were going to be very different from how you had imagined them. And your arrival in Australia was a portent of things to come.

I heard all this, and more, from you commencing the day after the night that changed my life.

I turned over the page and braced for the next chapter.

That night seemed to give you permission to erase the boundaries that normally exist between mother and daughter, boundaries that should never be crossed.

The events of that night were so out of the ordinary that they left me wondering for days whether it had all been a bad dream.

Chapter 5

Late 1960s.

After reuniting with your husband in Australia, you had to learn quickly. He was not an easy person to get to know. Just when you thought you knew him, he would do something to make your head spin.

Like that night.

You know what I'm talking about, don't you.

But you don't like being reminded of it. Brings back too many bad memories, I guess.

You had both signed a contract, but within a few days, Dad had changed his mind. There were huge arguments between you: he wanted to pull out , but you insisted that was impossible.

Late one night, I was awoken by shouting outside my bedroom. Half asleep, I got up to see what the fuss was all about. There you were standing in the hallway with him facing you, a rifle at his side.

Seeing that this could go very bad very quickly, you pleaded with him.

"You signed the contract—we both signed it. I've talked to the lawyer. There's nothing to be done any more."

Being told that he couldn't do what he wanted to do by a woman was like a red rag to a bull.

"Get that contract annulled, otherwise you'll see what this rifle can achieve," he warned, raising the firearm and pointing it at you.

I was suddenly awake and on full alert. It all happened so quickly I didn't really think about how to react.

Instinctively I stepped out in front of you to shield you. I guess I thought he wouldn't shoot you if his daughter was standing in front of you.

But what happened next chained me to you for decades.

While I was staring intently at him, I suddenly felt a heaviness on my shoulders.

You had put your hands on my shoulders, holding me there. I was trapped, and I froze. My mind was blank and there was an enormous lump in my throat. My arms went limp and my legs nearly gave way beneath me as the impact of what was happening hit me.

I believed he'd shoot us both if we gave him cause. And I would be hit first.

From far away, I heard you say, "There's nothing I can do tonight. I'll make some calls in the morning."

He relaxed from his ready-to-attack position, lowered the gun and walked back into the voluminous bedroom. Placing the firearm on the floor underneath his side of the double bed, he stretched out, pulled the covers up to his chin and, within minutes, was snoring.

I turned to see you had gone ashen, your eyes full of fear. There was something else there too — resigned hopelessness.

Your eyes told me that you held little or no hope that his demands could be met.

I was shaking as I walked back to my bedroom. It was only a few feet, but it felt like a mile. In bed, I tossed and turned for what seemed like hours, unable to get the image of the gun in my father's hands out of my head.

The next morning when I got up, I wondered whether it had all been a nightmare. The look in your eyes told me it wasn't.

No blood was spilled in that place, neither immediately following that event, nor at any other time. Still, deep wounds, invisible to the eye, appeared that night.

Not only was there the threat of you and I being killed by my own father, but your hands on my shoulders signalled to me that I was your shield.

When I reflect on that time as an adult, I realise that that was the night when the fog began rolling in.

In the beginning though it was more like a mist.

I went to school the next day, and every day after

that, dazed, an empty shell.

Had it really happened? Or was it just a bad dream? It felt surreal. Things seemed to happen in slow motion. And I always felt I was standing on the edge of a precipice, unable to breathe.

Coming home the next day I found you sitting at the kitchen table, like you were waiting for me. You had made *biscotti*, and you asked me to sit with you. I was expecting you to explain Dad's actions from the night before, to try to soothe me. But you didn't. All you did was cry and pour out your fears to me.

Every day after school was like this.

For weeks I waited for the axe to fall.

Each morning I felt relief to be going to school, to be leaving the turbid swamp of emotions fomenting in the house. The air was so thick with unspoken hopes and fears and bottled-up emotions, you could cut through it with a knife.

Each afternoon, as the hands of the clock ticked over towards going-home time, I felt the dread rise inside me from the pit of my stomach, a serpent coiling itself around my heart and throat, tightening my breathing and strangling any utterance I might make about what troubled me.

Questions raced endlessly around in my head: Would you still be alive when I returned home from school? Would I find you dead in a pool of blood?

Frightened to go home each day, I became very protective of my younger siblings. They were too young to understand what was going on, but I thought I understood. I understood that my father would kill you if you didn't achieve the outcome he so desperately wanted, and that we children would be left motherless. It didn't matter to me that we would also be left without a father. In fact, the thought of being fatherless was a relief.

What father would threaten to kill his wife and leave his children orphans to get what he wanted? I just could not understand that.

With all the sophistication of a twelve-year-old, I developed a plan in my head for just this possibility. If I came home and found you dead, I would call a taxi, grab the younger ones, and go to your parents' place.

Through the days and weeks that followed, I became increasingly vigilant, always watching out for what might happen next. As time drew closer for him to arrive home from work each day, I grew more anxious, so I couldn't concentrate on my homework. A menacing sense of foreboding became my constant companion, triggered by the hands of the clock showing an hour till his return.

I struggled to put on a happy face, as you demanded. I knew it would help you, yet all the while I felt like I'd swallowed molten lead.

I struggled to sit down to dinner with this man who had put the whole family at risk, yet to avoid making things worse I did.

I stuffed down the food, hardly tasting what I ate, in the hope it would stop the burning sensation in my stomach. I ate what you told me to, as much as you told me to, so I wouldn't draw attention to myself. I became very good at that—not drawing attention to myself. I went under the radar, trying to make myself invisible. Over time I became 'Miss Goody Two-Shoes' to the outside world. Inside—that was something else. Doing anything that drew attention to myself was suicide, I believed.

Years later, when I was an adult, you told me that the crisis had been settled. Dad got his way.

At the time, though, I never knew when it was over.

You kept on pouring your heart out to me. Even when the crisis came to an end, you didn't stop.

For me, the crisis never ended.

Chapter 6

Do you know what my experience of growing up was like?

You never asked me, so I don't expect you do. Let me tell you now.

I always felt tied up in knots inside. It was always, in all ways, a catch-22. No matter what I did, or how I did it, I was never good enough. And of course, being a female was never as good as being a male.

Male children were the only 'good' children to have. As a female, I was clearly born defective. Or was it that, in Sicilian culture, females were considered a burden to families?

How do I express to you how never being good enough felt for me?

Sometimes it's just easier to avoid thinking about it, but avoiding it doesn't make it go away.

To make sure that I was as unproblematic for you as possible as an adolescent and a young adult, you began controlling me, starting around the time I became your confidante.

You controlled, what I wore, how I walked, how I talked, my posture, who I associated with, even at school, where I went, who I saw, who my friends were, how I spent my time, what I did around the house. Even when I was at university and I wanted to meet some friends for coffee in town, you refused to allow me to go, because only 'flighty, cheap' girls did that sort of thing. You wanted to keep an eye on me all the time, so I spent many weekends and holidays helping you around the house, cooking, baking, spring cleaning while much of the time, I was on the verge of spontaneous combustion.

All those years you told me that it was your responsibility to make sure I maintained *due piede in un stivale* (two feet in one boot), that I stayed on the straight and narrow, until I married. I had to be pure, chaste, unstained, untouched, uncorrupted for a future husband to find me acceptable and to honour my parents.

But it wasn't just about me being 'acceptable'. It was also about clearing the path for my sister Maria. If I married well, with your approval, then the chances of Maria being found 'acceptable' by a future husband and getting a 'good' husband were also high.

That was medieval thinking to me. All I could do was shake my head in disbelief.

I wasn't interested in marrying someone who needed a woman who had been raised in that fashion.

I was growing up in a western society during the 1960s and 1970s, a period of massive social change. Yet you and Dad, and all your family, and other Sicilian families in Australia were living in the dark ages, where there were two sets of rules: one for men, and another for women.

Many Sicilian girls socialised among themselves and with other Sicilian families. They met at the Italian

Club for dances and other social events. I, on the other hand, wasn't allowed. I couldn't socialise with Australian friends, and I couldn't make any friends in the Italian community or even in the church community. My life centred on school and home.

I often wondered how I would ever meet anyone I could even consider marrying.

How many times did I ask you the one question you had no answer for: "If I'm not allowed to go anywhere or meet anyone, or have any social life whatsoever, how do you suppose I am ever going to meet someone who could possibly become my husband? And even if I did meet someone, how would I know if he was the one?"

You had no answers, only proverbs and homilies that you had received as a young girl from your own ancestors.

I know now that you were talking from a place of imprisonment. The best you could do was try to comfort a fellow prisoner with empty words that you hoped would convince me not to do anything 'stupid', like elope or run away from home, and hope and pray that somehow 'God' would bring me a 'good marriage'.

As I made my way through uni, the veil of ignorance that had once masked the truth began to lift and I could no longer accept your platitudes.

You gave me some beauties back then, Mum, like: "God will look after you. He will bring you a husband, *si Dio vuole* (God willing)."

I was nineteen when I rejected the Catholic faith that I had been raised in.

I needed answers. I needed to know that there was a way through the hell that I was in, that there was a light at the end of the tunnel. Catholicism only gave me more of what you were serving up — vapid banalities with a side dish of guilt. For 'sweets', you offered 'you can do whatever you like after marriage' while Catholicism offered 'resurrection of the dead' as its version of 'living happily ever after'. Your cultural beliefs and your religion were two sides of the same coin.

You couldn't offer me any hope, any consolation, or even any compassion.

Dad was your gaoler, and you were mine. And thus the prison created by the patriarchal family belief system was complete and hermetically sealed. The only way out of the prison was via an 'acceptable' marriage... or death.

There were times when the latter looked very appealing. But I rejected both options, and always looked for a third way.

There must be another way became my mantra. It was the only thing that kept me from succumbing to suicidal thoughts, or thoughts of marriage Sicilian style, a fate I considered to be worse than death.

I needed you, I hated you, I felt sorry for you, but I needed support, and you gave me none.

You put me in a cage where you could keep an eye on me all the time, where you could keep tabs on me and make sure I didn't wander off the straight and narrow.

You told me it was for my own good.

I knew though that it was for the honour of the whole clan. By marrying *in pace* (with the family's consent and approval), I would ensure that all the young females in the extended family would have 'good marriages' later in life, because my 'honourable' marriage would mean that the whole clan was 'honourable'.

There, that's the crux of it: the needs of the group are more important than the needs of the individual.

I was expected to sacrifice my life to comply with the patriarchal rules and have a 'good marriage', so that the whole family's honour would be retained and all the other females in the family would have a chance at attracting a 'good marriage'.

No wonder everyone in your family, from your parents to your brothers, sisters, and their spouses, had an interest in my chastity! No wonder they asked you questions about me which I considered intrusive and none of their fucking business!

I was the first female of this new generation born outside Sicily. As a trailblazer, I would be made an example of, whether I did things 'right', or whether I didn't.

From the time I was eleven years old, you ordered me to stay on the straight and narrow. You even went so far as to threaten me with banishment from the family if I became pregnant before marriage... at eleven.

As for you, I'd seen Dad beat and threaten you enough times to know that he was capable of killing you if he felt his honour compromised. Your job was to keep me pure and chaste so that you and your husband could hold your heads high in your community and not lose face in your family and social groups. If you failed to do your job properly, that would make you a bad mother, causing Dad to lose face among his friends. He couldn't afford to be cuckolded by his wife, or humiliated by his daughter. And he put onto you the responsibility of raising his children so that he would not lose face by our actions.

Well, hallelujah!

It was always about you and what you needed. You and Dad needed not to lose face, not to feel ashamed of me, not to be isolated by your community, or derided by your peers. You thought you had it tough, coming to a country where you couldn't speak the language, where you didn't know anyone; where there were no services for new migrants. I know it wasn't easy for you, but you had work, you had a home, you met and made friends, and most of all, you had your family here for emotional support.

I had no emotional support, from anyone, for anything.

At times I felt splintered into a million little pieces, living one life outside home and another life inside the home.

At school and college, I had to live according to the norms and rules of western society that valued the individual over the group. That meant making my own independent decisions.

At home, I had to live by ancient patriarchal rules that valued group survival over survival of the individual. Individual needs, wants, dreams had to be suppressed for the good of the group. So I had to defer to and ask permission of you and Dad for everything, even when I was twenty-one years of age and legally an adult.

Do you know how that made me feel?

I felt worthless... because I often got it wrong, both inside and outside the home. I felt frustrated that I couldn't understand the rules. Outside the home, rules and norms were clearer, and I came to understand them. There was more tolerance and forgiveness and more clearly defined boundaries. But I never felt that I belonged to any group outside the home.

I didn't feel I belonged in the Sicilian group either. I didn't seem to 'get' the rules. I didn't get the way the rules seemed to change, without warning, and I often didn't know what the rules were until I had breached them. It was like a minefield that I constantly had outdated maps for. In fact, I often had no maps at all for the minefield that imprisoned me.

It was all so chaotic, so set up in favour of those with power in the family — Dad. He had to be pacified. If he wasn't content, I never knew what he would do. He was a rage-a-holic, and I never knew what would set him off. It wasn't alcohol as it was for many other men.

Over those years, all I could put it down to were his frustrations and his inability to regulate his emotions. He was a proud Sicilian man whose role in life was to work and provide for his family. In return, he expected loyalty, respect, and total obedience from his wife and children. It was my job as his daughter to make him proud, and I was to do that by not questioning his authority, not questioning his rules and norms, and blindly obeying him.

At the age of twenty, I had undertaken some asser-tiveness training at college. That was the big thing at the time, and many girls were doing it to protect themselves.

One evening I decided to put the training to the

test. I told you and Dad that I was going to the movies with a girlfriend after dinner. She was coming to pick me up and would drop me off afterwards. Dad said nothing, did nothing. His face was totally expression-less. He gave nothing away. Do you remember? Since he didn't react, I thought it would be ok. I was twenty after all!

When I returned home, I went straight to bed. Next morning, you told me what had happened after I left.

Dad had demanded to know where I was going, even though I had told him before I left. Before you had a chance to reply, he warned, "If anything happens, I will throw both of you, mother and daughter, over the balcony of this building onto the street below."

That was from the top of a five-storey building.

Assertiveness training, clearly, was not the solu-tion to my problem.

I remember you telling me about a time in the early years of your marriage when you had sewn a dress for yourself. He didn't like the dress, for reasons he never shared with you, and he forbade you from wearing it again. Like most young women, you loved wearing the fashion of the day. Being unfamiliar with his ways, though, you thought nothing of wearing it again.

Next time you put it on, he threatened to put a match to it while you wore it.

In the late '60s, as a young teenager, you made me a dress with a halter neckline and cut out sleeves. The fabric was in a multi-coloured pop art design, and was flared from the neck down. It was the height of fashion at the time, and I loved it.

The very first time I wore it though, he told me to take it off and never wear it again. I knew from the tone of his voice that he meant it. I never wore it again—at least that's what he believed.

It wasn't that the dress was outrageous or immodest. God forbid!

He just didn't like it. It was the same with all my clothes. I'd never know what he didn't like until I actually wore it, and till then, I'd be on tenterhooks.

I kept the dress at the back of my wardrobe. It saw the light of day some time later.

With these sorts of things happning, it's little wonder I felt out of place, as if I didn't belong anywhere.

I was stuck in that space where two diametrically opposed worlds intersect: My very own 'no man's land'.

I had to figure out how I could succeed in or at least play these worlds, to get what I wanted.

Slowly, over time, I began to figure things out, but not before I had made quite a few mistakes.

At first, I tried rebelling, and I was good at it. I questioned everything: all the norms, all the rules, all the dictates and whimsical decisions. I raged a lot in my teenage years. I was outraged by the unfairness. Other people's needs, adults' needs, were always more important than my needs, more important than me. One minute you treated me as your equal and your confidante, the next minute you treated me as your property, an object, weighed down with your often unspoken expectations.

I was a confused and very angry teenager, angry that I was watched, controlled, manipulated, threatened, dumped upon, put down, shamed, and imprisoned, yet still expected to fulfil the family's expectations to a high standard without question, and with a smile.

After a lifetime of gut-wrenching soul-searching, I can now see the pattern of abuse that I was subjected to.

Keeping me imprisoned in a cage was as much for your safe-keeping as it was for mine. For, if I brought dishonour on Dad and the family, it was clear that I would be banished from the family home. Your punishment would have been death, or at the very least, a violent beating.

He would have avenged his 'honour'.

He was crazy enough to do it.

But in the process, both you and Dad made me responsible for whether you lived or whether you died.

You both made me responsible for whether my siblings would grow up orphans. You laid that responsibility squarely on my shoulders, from the tender age of eleven, and you repeated it continually over the next ten years.

You, and Dad, and your whole family misused me.

I put my pen down and walk away from my writing. The emotions from the past catch up with me again and overwhelm me. I need a break.

When I return to the desk, cup of steaming black coffee in hand, I pick up the thread.

I know you were lonely through your marriage, Mum, but I was even lonelier. While you treated me as your confidante and got things off your chest, I talked to no one. You drilled into me that I was to tell no one what was going on inside our family. This was our family secret, and it had to be kept that way.

Your rule for me, Mum, was *due piede in un stivale*. To this day I remember it very clearly.

My hand quivered. Tears slid down my face onto the page, like bombs dropping onto barren land, or meteors crashing into the moon, leaving behind impact splashes, and creating moist craters in the paper.

I was so young, so impressionable, so vulnerable, and so needy. I didn't need threats; I needed your love, support and understanding. I didn't need bans; I needed education.

In what, you might ask?

Do you think that at age eleven I had any idea how babies were made? I thought I could get pregnant even if I was kissed by a boy. How was I supposed to know? You told me nothing. There was no sex education at school, there was not even a hint of talk about sex in public, it was not something discussed in polite company, or in front of children.

So if I didn't know how babies were made, how could I know what to do?

More importantly, how could I know what *not* to do?

You thought I would just *know*, did you?

How? I ask you. How?

I lived in a place of deep, dark, silent terror where I believed that being kissed by a boy would leave me pregnant.

Let me tell you about the first time that I received any information about the facts of life.

When I was in eighth grade, my home economics teacher was expecting. Close to the end of her pregnancy, I took her aside and asked her quietly how the baby was born. I was horrified.

Uuuugggggghhhhh, I thought. Then, when I had collected myself a little, I asked her how the baby got in there in the first place, and she looked at me in disbelief, and just said, "The same way it comes out."

Well, that started my head spinning. How on earth could a baby get inside a woman's body?

It just so happened that she was my biology teacher as well, and she reminded me of the basics of reproduction. But what had me totally confused was, how did the sperm get inside the woman's body to meet the egg and start reproducing itself?

Come, tell me, was this the 'dirty' secret of intimacy that you had to be an adult to know about?

Why did you threaten to banish me if I got pregnant when I didn't even know how pregnancy came about? You needn't have worried about that. I found the whole idea repulsive at that age.

But it seems this was your biggest worry as I was growing up. And from where I was standing, sometimes your child and sometimes your confidante, you were worried not so much for my sake, but for yours and for your family's reputation. You were more concerned about the shame that you and Dad would confront than you were about what a teenage pregnancy and banishment would do to me.

That's what angered me the most... that your reputation and the family's mattered more than I did.

You gave me no information to protect myself

with, yet you threatened me with exile if I strayed or stepped outside the 'boot'.

Did it never cross your mind that educating me would have been more effective than threatening me?

Did you never stop to consider what those threats of ostracism were doing to me, day in, day out?

I was always a 'rebel', you told me.

I questioned your practices and traditions. I wanted the same opportunities as others to socialise, so that made me a 'wild child', ready to try anything, did it?

I see now that that was the reason for the threats of expulsion, the manipulation, the control.

Why? Why didn't you put my interests before your own?

Why did you put me in front of you as your shield, to protect yourself?

Is this what the Catholic Church teaches? As far as I recall, the church teaches protection of the weak and vulnerable. But there was no sign of religious principles here in this family.

Don't trust anyone outside the family! That was the family mantra. No, we couldn't trust anyone outside the family with our dirty little secrets, could we? They would have gleaned every little detail they could about us and our sordid family tale, and then gossiped and gloated to their hearts' content, wouldn't they? And then they would have held me up as a negative role model to their daughters!

No, don't trust anyone outside the family. They will exploit our story mercilessly. You don't know who you can trust outside. There are threats and dangers and risks lurking everywhere outside the family.

What you didn't tell me was that the biggest danger was not outside the family. It was *inside* the family. When I figured that out was when I really began to rebel.

You tried so hard to control me. And the harder you tried to manipulate me, the more I rebelled.

You, who called yourselves Roman Catholics, who were supposed to protect the young, the weak and the vulnerable, you put a defenceless child at risk.

You, who thought of yourselves as a close-knit family, created the appearance of cohesion for public consumption, but underneath there was trauma, distress, anxiety, terror, simmering rage, and death threats.

You, who thought of yourself as a good mother, were tying me up in knots with confused loyalties and confusing roles.

You were hypocritical, saying one thing and doing another. How I hated you for that! How I hated Dad for putting you in this crazy double-bind position.

I just didn't want to be there. I'd had enough of gut-wrenching fear. By the time I reached my mid-teens, I had worked out how not to be there.

Chapter 7

By the time I was in year eleven, the 1970s had begun. The 1960s, particularly the last years of the decade, witnessed tumultuous social change. The decade had begun with the promise of prosperity in western nations, including Australia. World War II brought an end to social class in Europe, and whatever remained of the old feudal system disappeared. The middle class expanded throughout western nations, and by the mid-1960s, many working-class people in those nations could afford a radio, tele-vision, refrigerator, and motor vehicle. The worldwide trend in the 1960s was one of prosperity, expansion of the middle class, and new technology. Socially, this economic trend brought with it a levelling out of social classes, a belief in equal opportunity for all, a desire for greater individual freedom and the democratisation of social and educational institutions.

Cultures that had been rigid weren't able to meet the demands for greater individual freedom. Young people in these cultures broke free of the social constraints imposed by previous generations by questioning and rebelling. Many western nations experienced civil unrest with students rioting in the streets of major cities in Europe, America, and Australia, the most notable being the student revolt in Paris in May 1968.

As the war in Vietnam raged, and still had some way to go, the desire for peace after decades of war was growing. Civil disobedience and anti-war marches on the streets of major cities around the world became increasingly frequent and violent. The Beatles were singing their way around the world, changing everyone's ideas of what good music was, even though many of your generation thought they brayed like oxen.

The contraceptive pill had taken the world by storm, and women felt no longer bound by history, traditional social roles, or society's expectations. Women were freeing themselves of the chains imposed on them by male-dominated society and the sexual revolution had begun in earnest in the western world. Freedom to choose your own life and your own path was the main theme of the times, not just for men, but for women as well. These things were happening in Brisbane too.

You and Dad had other ideas for your daughter though. None of those changes touched our family, as though we were stuffed inside some time capsule, or locked away in some underground nuclear bomb shelter, safe from the lunacy of the outside world.

Safe, under the watchful control of the warden.

I would tell you about other Sicilian girls who were allowed out with their friends; they would go to the movies, to dances, to one another's homes.

That's ok for them; it's not ok for you, you told me.

Somehow, different rules applied to me, and I just didn't get it.

I wanted freedom — like everyone else.

And while I couldn't put it into words at that time, more than anything I wanted freedom from the fear that gnawed away silently yet persistently at my insides. I wanted freedom from the rage I felt at being chained up, not for what I had done, but for what you thought could happen. I felt smothered, imprisoned, watched by everyone in the family.

There was one Italian girl in my class in high school. She was everything I wanted to be. She was attractive, popular, easy-going, and she laughed easily and a lot. Oh God, how I wanted to be as carefree as she was. She had beautiful almond-shaped eyes, and when she chatted with someone, she made them feel as though they were the most important person in the world for her at that moment. And she was allowed out.

You were not impressed that I was friends with her. You said she was not raised the same as I was, and that I shouldn't expect to be allowed out, just because she was.

Over time, I found myself drawn to Eloise more

and more, as things got worse at home. I often wondered if I could tell her what was going on in my home. I dared not. What could she tell me to do anyway? All the same, I sometimes felt I couldn't take my eyes off her when she was talking with others, when she was laughing, when she so confidently mixed with others.

I wanted her to pay attention to me, to make me feel special, but she mixed with everyone, oblivious to me, distributing her attention equally to all, like gentle rain falling indiscriminately to the ground. Her laughter tinkled across the classroom, and when I looked up, I could see her sharing a joke or a story with her group of friends. How I longed to be like her.

We finished high school, and she never knew that I loved her.

Or maybe I just envied her.

I was frustrated by what was going on at home, but I was changing as well. Every which way I turned there was a brick wall, and as I progressed in my teens, those brick walls seemed to close in on me, relentlessly, centimetre by centimetre. There seemed to be no way out.

That didn't stop me from imagining a way out, or from believing that there was another way.

When in Year 8, I played the position of defence goalie in the school's netball team. My team won all at-home games that season, and we made it into the regional semi-finals. The semi-final game was held on a Saturday afternoon at an all-girls Catholic school in the centre of town. As I'd taken part in all the games up until then, I had no reason to think I wouldn't be able to attend.

In the late 1960s Brisbane city was a ghost town on a Saturday afternoon, as you might remember. All shops closed at noon, and by 12.30, the streets were empty, except those up to no good, you believed.

As I was getting ready to go to the game, you told me to 'go to bed', your euphemism for 'you're not going anywhere'. A young girl going to the city on her own on a Saturday afternoon was asking for trouble, you told me. And you didn't allow me to go. There were no mobile phones, no mums sharing the pick-up and delivery of children, and no way to let anyone know before the game.

The following Monday, Sister Loretta, the team coach, tore shreds off me, accusing me of being unreliable. I tried to explain that you didn't allow me to go to the game, but she wouldn't listen.

It wouldn't have made any difference anyway. I had been unreliable.

Once.

Unreliable people don't get a second chance.

She removed my name from ever being on the basketball team again.

My team lost that Saturday afternoon—the first time that season. Maybe we would have lost anyway, even if I'd been there. But I did wonder how much my absence had to do with it.

Years later, you admitted to me that the main reason you hadn't allowed me to go was what Dad would have said or done that afternoon if I hadn't been at home. Yet, you had allowed me to attend all previous games on Saturday afternoons that season.

Explain that for me, will you, Mum?

I was in high school. I hadn't heard of Viktor Frankl, the Jewish psychiatrist who survived Nazi concentration camps in the 1940s by finding purpose and meaning in that experience. He realised that even in prison, people have the freedom to choose how they react to extreme situations; if we hold onto some lifeline, we can endure almost anything.

I was learning how to survive this no-man's land whose maps you changed as you went along.

There must be another way, I kept telling myself, willing it to be so.

One night, I must have been around sixteen years old, I couldn't stand it any more. I wiped away my all-too-frequent tears of frustration and rage and decided to just leave the house. I wanted to feel the cool night air on my skin, I wanted to know what it felt like to be out on my own at night, I wanted to know what it felt like to be free and not afraid. But heck, I was going out alone at night, a young girl. Sure, I was scared, but the excitement of doing it was stronger than my fear.

Being born male would have made my life a lot easier. How many times I wished I'd been born a boy. Going out of the house at night alone wouldn't have been such a drama then.

But I wasn't born male.

I was a female growing up in a patriarchal family from a land far away in accordance with customs and beliefs adhered to and handed down from generation to generation and a time too long ago to remember.

The two worlds, inside and outside the home, clashed often for me, made worse by Dad's jealousy, unpredictable violent rages, aggression, and misogyny, your constantly creating and revising the rules to suit yourselves, and by your traumatising me by sharing with me your fears and whispers of those things that happen between a husband and wife.

Do you know how many times I wished him dead, just so we could live in peace?

Do you know how many times I prayed that he wouldn't kill you, Mum?

Years later you told me that you didn't think I would remember such things.

How could I *not* remember such things? How did you think I might remember 'school' things but forget 'home' things?

You had no answer for that.

As I write this letter, Mum, I feel enormous pressure inside me. I want to write, yet at the same time I avoid it. I feel there is so much to say, and it can only come out one word at a time, one page at a time, like an overfull bag of thick icing being wrung out through a narrow nozzle.

This is how I feel. If I write, I feel this pressure; if I don't write, I feel the pressure, and somewhere at the back of my mind, a phrase keeps going around and around in my head: this is the path to freedom. And when I have emptied my mind and my emotions onto the page, I will be truly emptied and free of the stuff I have been carrying around with me for half a century. These pages are not just a dumping ground for my 'stuff'; the act of dumping my psyche onto paper reveals to me what is in there, and helps me to organise it, file it away, and archive it, so it won't ever blow up in my face again, unexpectedly, like unexploded ordnance.

So I sit here on a Friday night and write this letter to you, not for you, but for me, so I can finally move on. I never thought I could write about my thoughts, my feelings, my experiences growing up with you in your family. This is the path to freedom for me, and as the words appear on the paper, there is a slight easing in my gut, but knowing that there is still so much more to write, the pressure doesn't ever really go away. I sit here, tired, feeling under pressure, trying to make sense of it all, but it doesn't come out in any particular order or sequence. I just have to get it down as it comes.

Chapter 8

Into the Void

By the time I was fourteen years of age, I felt a huge void where my gut should have been. It was an indescribable emptiness that filled my body and my soul. Worst of all, I didn't know how to relieve it. It was achingly present all the time. I couldn't run away from it; it went with me wherever I went. It didn't abate when I flew into one of my rages followed by uncontrollable sobbing. It didn't even go away when I stuffed the void full of food. That just made me feel and look worse.

Where did that feeling of desolation and desperate emptiness come from? If I knew where it came from, maybe I could make it to go away?

I didn't know it then, but these were the naïve

thoughts of a lost adolescent going deeper and deeper into a world cut off from the outside world.

By this time, Dad had nothing more to do with me. He didn't speak to me, but by God I knew he was watching me.

You weren't there for me. You weren't interested in my life, what I thought or felt, what my dreams and aspirations were, what if any problems I had.

I was there for you though, as you downloaded your deepest darkest thoughts, feelings, and fears to me.

I was your pressure release valve; you got it out of your system and dumped all the vitriol, the hatred, despair, and fear, all onto me... and then you committed me to silence, forbidding me from ever whispering a word of it to anyone.

Sometimes I wondered if there was anyone in the family I could have talked to. There was your mother, *Nonna* Maria. She was no help at all. I thought she was a friend to the family, but I learned that she was the one behind the way things were in our family.

As the matriarch, she was highly critical of you and me for even the slightest infraction.

Who else was there? Your sisters? With their husbands, I sensed that they had challenges of their own.

It seemed to me that all the women were run by the same programs of shame, abuse, and silence.

And my life was shaping up to be like theirs... except for my academic achievements. That was the way out of home, the path to freedom.

You told me often enough that you had no control over anything in your life either. When you were growing up, everyone was in the same position; everyone was raised much the same.

But this was different.

Now, we lived in a society that valued freedom of the individual to choose their own life and make their own decisions, for better or for worse, for women as well as for men.

Independence? Freedom? Personal agency?

For others maybe. Not for me.

No, my life was strictly controlled, to eliminate, or at least minimise, the possibility, however remote, of being 'touched' by a man.

I even had no control over my body that was changing without my knowledge or consent. Not knowing that the changes were normal, I felt ashamed of my body and tried to hide it.

I didn't want Dad to see it; I didn't want any male members of the extended family to see it. No matter, they saw, they observed, they whispered among themselves. As I learned later, they talked among themselves much like the old women did in Sicily, sitting at the front of their houses in the sun, knitting or darning the well-worn socks of husbands, sons, and brothers, watching passers-by, watching out for any strangers. And criticising anyone, any *woman*, who did not conform to the strict unspoken rules of the village. Even someone who did not wear the modest (ie 'drab') dress code of the village was soundly criticised as being a tramp, or worse.

I couldn't put words to it then, but I know now that it was my body that they were all watching for any signs of having been 'touched' by a male before marriage.

It didn't matter what the men did though. The family's reputation always rested on the shoulders of the women. And if they fell, so too did the family's reputation.

God Almighty, this belief is older than Christianity itself!

I know you believe you were justified in your extreme protection of me, but where did you think the threat was coming from?

Unless... there really was a need to be extremely protective of me.

Unless... you believed the threat could come from anywhere anytime... like your own older sister who eloped in the late 1940s, causing shame and scandal in your family.

What happened to her could happen to anyone. Is that what you thought?

To prevent it from happening in your own family, all the women in your family ganged up to ensure my complete adherence to the code.

Can't have the next generation bringing shame on the family, can we? That would have been *proof* that the family was no good, like apples that are shiny and red on the outside, but rotten at the core.

No, we must ensure that all the apples are perfect, both inside and out, so that the men who 'buy' them at marriage get what they think they are buying.

Per l'onore della famiglia, for the family honour.

This was a nightmare I thought I'd never wake up from.

The only way I could keep my sanity was to keep believing that there was another way out.

Even the Catholic nuns who were my teachers were echoing ideas similar to those at home. In high school, the nuns preached that young girls were like peaches that bruised easily through touch. They also told us that should we find ourselves in a situation of being raped, it was better to die than to be raped, so we could enter the Kingdom of Heaven pure.

Hell, I just couldn't get away from it.

All the girls in my class laughed it off.

I didn't.

It was not just the men who saw what was going on, out of the corner of their eyes. They also talked at work sites. They talked about girls who were suitable for marriage, and those who weren't.

All the females, the mothers and the grand-mothers, the aunts and the older (female) cousins, worked together, as they had always done throughout history, to make sure the next generation of females grew up by the code, lived by the code, married by the code, forever and ever. The old women were the strongest observers and servants of this code, preserving and perpetuating it through the way they raised their children, both male and female.

That was how the children had always been raised in your culture. It preserved stability and gave a sense of security to everyone adhering to the code. As restrictive as it was, people believed it was better to adhere to the code and be part of the group, than not to adhere to the code and be cast out where survival was at risk. And they made sure that individuals believed that their survival was threatened outside the group.

The code was the cement that bonded the society together, enabling communities to survive as a unit against outside threats.

The women ensured the community's survival by preserving the traditional child-raising practices, while the men sat back, earned an income, sometimes meagre, sometimes not, in the knowledge that the women were taking care of things at home to ensure stability.

If change was to happen, it would have to come through the women. Men had too much to lose. And it would not be the generation that migrated that would change. It would be the second and third generations that would change these beliefs and customs.

It didn't matter that you now lived on a different

continent, in a different society with values and traditions different from your own, in a different time, and far away from the home you grew up in. You all came with your home within you, in your heads, in your hearts, and that was what you wanted to pass on to me. But that was as remote to me as the moon. I had no connection to your village life and its ways. In fact, I came to despise it. I rejected your culture at that stage of my life, but how can you reject something that is a part of you? I was still attached to it. I was rejecting part of myself as an adolescent, but I didn't realise it for many years.

The void in me was getting deeper with each passing month, each passing year. With no one to talk to, with my movements controlled, with no light at the end of the tunnel, I became increasingly aloof and desperate for a way out, or for a pressure release valve.

Since the night that had changed my life, when I thought you and I were going to die, the uncertainty of when, or if, you would die at his hands never ended. He was chaotic and erratic, mocking you one minute, thundering the next.

From that night on, I was captive to your ancestral beliefs and traditions that were as old, worn, and unyielding as the Sicilian landscape itself.

Chapter 9

Floundering through adolescence, working hard at school, fantasising about my escape, hearing more and more about how your life was, how bad things were for you during the war and post-war period, I didn't really care any more.

You worked very hard to make my life a mirror image of your own. You needed me to be just like you: to live like you, to think like you, to behave like you.

Only that way could you control the worst that life might throw at me and keep me safe.

And while you worked hard at making me a clone of you, I met your efforts with just as much resistance.

I argued with you, found flaws in your arguments and smashed them, but none of that made any difference. We were talking about archaic beliefs that you clung to like a drowning person clings to a reed.

Those beliefs were beyond rational examination.

What began as rational discussion always ended up in a huge row between us, with you uttering the fatalistic words: *Così è*, this is how it is.

Si Dio vuole, ti porta un buon matrimonio. God willing, you will have a good marriage.

Was I interested in marriage at fifteen, sixteen, or seventeen?

Hell no!

I was interested in meeting people, going to the movies, taking part in netball comps, and just hanging out with friends. Like everyone else... not segregated and isolated. And because I was cut off from everyone else, I had nothing to share with them at school, no experiences I'd had on the weekend that I could share on Monday morning. Everyone saw me as dull and boring, and they kept their distance. No one wanted to be seen hanging out with a deadbeat.

Get a life, they used to say.

Sure!

As I got older, I observed Filip more and more, and it began to dawn on me that having fights and arguments at home with you changed nothing. On the other hand, Filip was quiet at home, said very little, kept to himself, and jealously protected his privacy. Then he went out and did what he wanted to do.

Ever so gradually an idea crept up on me.

It wasn't just big; it was huge!

All this time I had been thinking that I was a prisoner to your medieval beliefs and traditions around women, marriage, and family, and that in order to stay alive, and keep you alive, I had to stay on the straight and narrow, *con due piede in un stivale*.

I began wondering.

What if it was you and Dad who were actually the captives?

Dad wouldn't banish me if I didn't get pregnant

before marriage.

And he wouldn't kill you if I didn't get pregnant.

I began to see that you were a prisoner to your need to be seen as a family of good repute. And Dad was a prisoner to his need to be seen in the Sicilian community as an 'honourable' man.

Both you and Dad were at the mercy of your *paesane*, countrymen, and wider family, who would not hold back from humiliating you if anything went off course.

Do you remember in the 1960s, when all those weddings, christenings, and confirmations took place in the family? In a Sicilian family, these were the events around which family life revolved.

I remember my brother Tony's christening, which took place when I was twelve. The christening was on a Sunday morning after Mass at the local parish church. His godparents and other invited guests came home for lunch. There must have been more than twenty people for lunch. And you had prepared all the food in the days before, a three-course Italian meal with pasta, mains and salad, then coffee.

And for once, I was glad there were so many people there — it took the focus off me for a little while. I sat back and watched everyone as they ate... whooooaaaa, I had never seen so many people eat so much food so quickly. One middle-aged woman stuffed her face with food, then chewed with her mouth open, so that oil and juices dribbled down her chin from the corner of her mouth. It was disgusting, but I was simply transfixed. I had never seen people eat like that, as if they'd never seen food before. And loud... lots of noise, the clinking of glassware and cutlery, lots of talking and laughter, mixed in with the squelching of food being chewed. I had no idea what they were talking or laughing about. Lots of talk about the old country, about places they had been, people they had known twenty or more years before. And there was Dad, at the head of the table, like a Viking earl, performing his duty to family and guests contentedly refilling their glasses with wine, laughing, sharing a joke or a story. He was a completely different person from the person he was when they weren't there. I felt sheltered by the crowd around me, safe, anonymous, invisible.

I hated that day.

I hated posing for photographs and putting on a fake smile.

I hated smiling at the rellies.

I hated the pretence of love when I knew that there was none.

I felt like a hypocrite. The whole family was hypocritical. They called themselves Catholics, but they donned their religion like a coat whenever they went to church. The men and women wore their best outfits to church, and the women covered their heads with lacy black or white mantillas inside the church. Outside, the other one hundred and sixty-seven hours of the week, they flaunted their prejudices.

So much hypocrisy.

So much gluttony.

So much jealousy and pride.

So much competition between them showing off, who was better, richer, more successful.

Little kindness, tolerance, patience, love, and empathy.

What was the purpose of sending me to an all-girls Catholic secondary school? Did you think they would make me a 'good girl'?

You never could explain to me adequately what it meant to be a 'good girl'. What makes a girl good as opposed to bad?

You tried telling me that a good girl obeys her parents and does what her parents tell her to do, stays on the straight and narrow, is a virgin at marriage, and brings honour to her family by marrying with the consent of the parents and with peace in the family.

Bringing honour to her family... that always came up.

But what about truth and deception, honesty and

hypocrisy? Don't these have something to do with being 'good' or 'bad'?

I had to tell the truth to be good, but telling the truth would have been bad, so I had to maintain the deception and practise hypocrisy. Under your rules, I was never good, or good enough. I had to be 'bad' to be 'good'. No wonder I was confused.

Growing up, I was preoccupied by questions like, 'How the hell do I get out of here?' 'How am I going to survive this?'

Questions not usually pondered by teenagers.

How could I obey you, my parents, and do what you told me to do when I couldn't respect you; when you, my mother, sometimes treated me as your personal confessor, and other times as if I were a 'rebel'; and when my father used intimidation and death threats, told blatant lies to squirrel himself out of situations he didn't like, and told you and me both, that we were crazy when he disagreed?

If I couldn't respect people like that, did that make

me a 'bad girl'?

I used to think that being a 'bad girl' meant telling lies, being dishonest, hurting others.

I had started navigating my way between Scylla and Charybdis, a rock and a hard place. I came back to this place many times during adolescence.

Chapter 10

I thought that night was a one-off. That night that changed my life, when I was forced to choose between your life and mine.

Like in the movie *Sophie's Choice*.

In that film, Meryl Streep's character, Sophie, was forced to choose which of her two children would die immediately on entering the Nazi concentration camp in 1942, and who would continue to live in the camp. Sophie chose to sacrifice her seven-year-old daughter. The decision broke her heart, left her grieving and filled with guilt for the rest of her life. She took her own life a few years after the end of the war.

My decision wasn't a one-off. I didn't know it then,

but it was just the beginning of being forced to decide between your life and mine regularly and consistently for the next ten years.

By the time I had reached fifteen or sixteen, a deep dark fog had descended over me. I felt like the walking dead while forced to appear happy when Dad was around. I only felt extreme emotion... I felt rage a lot of the time. By then, I could see that my life had the foundations of being a re-run of your life and the lives of Sicilian women I knew. And I railed against that too, at the injustice of not being allowed to have my own life, my own opportunities, to live the life that I imagined for myself.

Most of the time, though, I felt numb inside.

My mood began swinging wildly from anger and outrage, to numbness and emptiness.

I began taking things, you know, pills, uppers and downers. I was taking uppers when I felt dead inside, just to feel something, and I began taking sedatives when I was outraged. At those times, I just didn't know how to calm myself down. I felt like I was going out of my body and out of my mind. I know now that this experience is called 'dissociating', and I began dissociating more and more.

I bought these pills with the money I earned on Saturday mornings working in the local deli. I always had a job at that time – not just for the money.

It got me out of the house. And it got me out of my head.

After a while, taking drugs only kept a lid on things for me.

I began going to my school friend Valerie's place on Saturday afternoons for a while. Remember? I told you we were getting together to study. The only reason you let me go to her place was because she lived within walking distance. If I'd had to catch a tram or a bus to get there, I wouldn't have been allowed.

Valerie and I would chat about this and that, sometimes getting back to history that we were supposed to be studying, but it was dry, and I just couldn't get my head around it. Why was it so important to know today which king reigned in England in 1280 and what he did? That meant nothing to me at the time.

One Saturday afternoon, from the nearby street came the deep-throated rumbling of a motorbike edging closer. Val and I began talking louder just to hear each other over the noise. It was so close it sounded as if it were in the next room. I felt the floorboards of the old timber Queenslander quiver beneath me. I had never experienced the floor shake like that—I'd always lived in houses with concrete floors.

Then suddenly the noise stopped. I looked around at Valerie and didn't know if she saw fear or excitement on my face.

"That's my brother. He just got home from work."

"What does he do?"

"He's an apprentice boilermaker."

"And the bike?" I asked.

I'd been curious about motorbikes and the people who rode them for some time. They seemed so free. They didn't seem to care about social norms about what to wear, how they looked, or how they got around. It didn't seem to matter to them that other people in society looked down at them, or that they didn't belong to such social groups. They had their own groups, they understood one another, and they looked out for one another. I thought they were cool back then. They represented what I was looking for: Freedom from restrictive social and family rules, and a community that would take you in and look out for you.

Looking at it from the outside though, I didn't know that they had their own rules for their gangs. It just looked like a life of freedom to me. Years later, I read the bestseller, *Zen and the Art of Motorcycle Maintenance*, which fanned my interest in motorbike culture.

So, here I was, a sixteen-year-old girl romanticising the life of the bikie.

I loved the black leather they wore. If I was going to be branded a rebel, I might as well play the part, I figured. What better way to do that than to turn up at home wearing black leather bike pants and jacket, black leather boots with five-inch heels, and makeup of smoky eye shadow and red lipstick! Now that really would give the rellies something to talk about!

Oh how I wanted to rebel!

Grease hadn't hit the screen yet, but Sandy's transformation from timid, pearl necklace, twinset-wearing 'good girl' to black-leather-clad vamp was how I dreamed of my own transformation.

*That would **really** set tongues wagging*, I thought.

You and I had many a fight about me wanting to wear black. For you, it was the colour of grief and mourning, so you thought it inappropriate for me to wear as an adolescent. Because it was prohibited, I wanted to wear it even more but you, and particularly Dad, forbade it. By the time I had turned twenty, I'd had enough of your dictating to me, and I bought some black clothes and wore them!

"Oh, he just got his motorbike licence a few months ago, then he bought this bike to get to and from work," said Valerie.

If you had known that I was at a home where there were 'bodgies' on motorbikes, I would have been in a lot of trouble. They were social outcasts; they were working-class people, and they were rebels. Your children would not repeat Dad's life — truanting from school, being led astray by other kids who were similarly up to no good and being removed from school.

Suddenly, the expression on her face changed.

"You know what," she continued almost in a whisper, "would you like to go for a ride on his bike?"

Before I could reply, she continued, "I'll ask him. He could take you on a whirl, just around the block..."

My jaw dropped. I didn't know what to say. My heart skipped a beat before leaping into top gear. It was one of those moments that were to become increasingly frequent during my adolescent years: deciding between what I should do based on what I knew you would expect of me, and what I wanted to do.

My heart pounded with anxiety and with the

thrill of doing something prohibited. I went weak at the knees. It was 'wrong' for me to do this. Yet it was also 'right'. Questions began racing through my head: what would you think? What would the rellies think if I was found out? What would Dad do?

Not only was I considering going on a motorbike with someone considered a social outcast, I was also considering going with a man, a stranger I'd never met.

Of course, I was to be protected from all males outside the family. They all only ever wanted one thing.

I was terrified.

In my head, these questions raced round and round, blurring into one another. They were hijacking my ability to decide.

I felt nailed to the floor, and I couldn't say anything.

"What do you think?" she egged me on.

"Have you been on the bike? Have you been out for a ride?" I asked hesitantly.

"Shit yeah," she responded without a second thought. "It's really great—you'll love it. Come on, take a chance..."

I wanted to do something different, something that would make me feel alive, something that would take away that feeling of numbness inside, of being responsible for your life and the lives of my siblings. I just wanted to do something that *I* wanted to do, even if it was just for a short time.

I wanted to stop being the 'good girl', the nice, responsible girl. Just for once, I wanted to do something you considered 'bad'. Just once.

Who could possibly find out about this? Who would see me around the block, here in the 'burbs on a sleepy Saturday afternoon? Mum didn't talk to anyone around here, so she'd never know anyway.

This was how I found myself thinking. I wanted to do this, but another thought stopped me: what would you do if you found out?

It was like two parts of me arguing in my head.

But heck, how would you or Dad ever find out, and for that matter, anyone else in the family?

So I agreed. Immediately, she flew out of the room and ran downstairs to tee it up with her brother.

In the meantime, I stayed in the room. I was in there alone long enough to reconsider my decision. What if someone saw me and told my parents? Would he have an extra helmet for me? Then no one would recognise me if they did see me.

Before I could talk myself out of it, she was back in the room telling me it was all organised. Her brother would take me on a short spin around the block.

Walking down the steps of her Queenslander to the garage where her brother stood beside his bike felt like the longest walk in my life. She introduced us — his name was Pete — and I saw that he wasn't much older than me. Shooting sidewards glances, Pete handed me a helmet.

"Here, put this on, just in case... " he advised.

I was already alert, but Pete's comment made me even more so as I sensed imminent threat.

"Just in case?" I asked. "In case what?"

"You know... in case somethin' happens. It'll protect your head."

I felt the tension in my body ease slightly.

Taking the helmet from Pete, I checked if there was a visor. There was.

I eased the helmet over my thick curly black hair and buckled the latch under my chin. It felt snug, as though he had bought the right size for his passenger. His sister Valerie?

"Hop on," he said.

"That's going to be a bit awkward with this dress," I said.

I was wearing the dress that Dad had forbidden me to wear, its cacophony of colour ensuring it wouldn't be easily forgotten. Flared from the neck down, it would blow right up into my face as we gathered speed. So much for modesty.

"Tuck it in under your thighs," he suggested. "You can hold onto the backrest there, but if you haven't been on a bike before, you'd better hang onto me. Wrap your arms around my waist... don't want you falling off, especially when we go 'round corners."

Wrap my arms around his waist? Not bloody likely. I'd chance it.

I got on the bike, tucked the dress under my legs, and lowered the visor on the helmet.

Pete put his helmet on and lowered the visor. As he turned on the ignition, the bike sparked to life with a loud guttural rumbling reminiscent of distant thunder.

"Remember," I said to him from behind, "only a few minutes and only around the block. We've still got work to do," I lied.

Valerie stood in the driveway of her house and waved. "Have fun!" she shouted.

I want to, I thought, but there was so much else going through my head. I wanted to have fun; I desperately wanted to do something you considered 'bad', but I was really scared to do so. With my luck, I thought, *I'll get caught. Then I'll really be in the shit.* I was so paralysed with fear that I couldn't enjoy it.

Holding onto the passenger backrest to secure myself, I looked around as Pete drove: familiar streets and houses, familiar people. But they looked back at us with consternation. We were disturbing the suburban Saturday afternoon peace and quiet with that noisy motorbike. More than that though, I could see them tut-tutting and shaking their heads at the sight of a bikie with a young girl dressed in a colourful summer dress, sandals, and helmet. Would they think we were a couple—the bad boy leading the innocent young girl astray? Imagining they were thinking that put a smile on my face and gave me a moment or two of respite from the fear.

It amused me to think what my rellies would say if they saw me now. I imagined the gossiping, the self-righteous chastising, the frothing. Everyone would have something to say.

Just as we began leaning into a corner, I felt myself slip on the bike, jogging me back into the present. Instinctively, I let go of the backrest and wrapped my arms around Pete's narrow waist for safety, as he had suggested. Clasping my hands together at the front, I was now pressed up against his black leather jacket. I knew what you would think about me being in this compromising position, but I felt that safety was more important than appropriateness at that moment.

The anxiety I felt about the 'immorality' of this situation escalated in milliseconds as we rounded the corner to return to Pete and Valerie's house. As we drove past a car that looked like Dad's, I looked over and saw it was him. Suddenly, my heart began pounding at a hundred miles an hour. *Just as well I had the visor down*, I thought. *He wouldn't recognise me. But he might recognise the dress.* It was an original creation because you had sewn it. My hands were clasped so tight I was sure my knuckles had turned white.

Get through this, I kept telling myself, *get through this and go home.*

As it turned out, Dad was returning home early from work that Saturday afternoon, and he didn't notice the girl on the back of the motorbike, let alone her bespoke dress. His daughter wouldn't be seen dead in that dress in public.

That was the first and last time I went riding a motorbike as a sixteen-year-old, although I did so again later in life. So much anxiety and fear paralysed me that afternoon that the adventure was simply not worth breaking the rules for.

You want to know why I'm telling you about it now?

It's because I want you to know the only way I could ever get anything I wanted was to do it behind your back. You put me in a position where I always had to make a choice between your life and mine. If I did the 'right' thing, you lived; if I did the 'wrong' thing, you died.

What sort of a choice is that? It was a prison I could never escape from.

Yes, it was your job to keep me safe. But you did this by putting me in a cage and throwing away the key. This magical key would then somehow fall into the hands of a suitor who would marry me and set me free, in your version of this nightmarish fairytale.

I was raised to believe that your life was more important than mine, and Dad's life was more important than yours. In this hierarchy, sons' lives were more important than daughters', and if push came to shove, sons' lives were more important than their own mothers' as well. I saw this myself in Sicily.

In this ancestral view, my life served only to honour you.

And if I became wilful and did not honour you as custom dictated, my life was considered insignificant and therefore I could be disowned, banished, or even extinguished.

It was to be another forty years before I finally freed myself from that cage.

Chapter 11

In retrospect, I see that while he brown-nosed those he considered his 'betters' and disparaged those he considered below him in social standing, Dad reserved his most vitriolic attacks for you.

You, the daughter of a property owner, represented what he hated most—the class that debased and humiliated those who were 'lesser' than them.

When he left Sicily to pursue his dreams, he took his beliefs about social class and his hatred of it with him and played them out in a new land with a classless society. Australia was populated by the descendants of 'victims' of a similar social order that had rejected the working classes forced into petty crime just to survive.

The irony was that he looked down his nose at

those same descendants who, like him, were victims of a social order that had made them second-class citizens.

There were times when Dad appeared 'normal' and generous - he would have given the shirt off his back for others, particularly people he considered friends. There were many times I saw him extend his generosity, and yours, to others... his generosity knew no bounds. It was the old Arab custom of hospitality. *Rispettu*, in Sicilian. Unfortunately though, his generosity and friendship were often not reciprocated.

There's one time I remember very clearly with your neighbours, Dave and Jenny, in Dad's later years. Dave was a shift worker, so when he was home during the day, he sometimes had conversations with Dad over the fence. Dad would usually then invite him to the house. They chatted for hours over stubbies of beer. Dad was in heaven, ordering you to make pizza with your homemade salsa and pickled olives. Dave was a novice food preserver and he was keen to learn how to preserve olives and prepare dried tomatoes. You, of course, never sat down to talk with the men. It was not customary for women to do that. When Dave expressed an interest in learning how to make Sicilian preserves, Dad offered your services to make them for him. Not just show him how to make them, nor just a kilo or two. Dad told him to buy a ten-kilo box each of olives and tomatoes, and you would make them for him.

I remember you telling me how upset you were when he told you of his magnanimous offer to the neighbours. But what were your options? If you declined to do it, he would have felt that you were making him look bad in front of his friends; he would have lost face and looked and felt like a *puddicinu*, a young chicken, unmanly, henpecked, and dishonoured. If you agreed, you'd be exhausted.

What to do?

Clearly, there was only one option—you had to take on the project. As I write these words, I remember you telling me the story as it unfolded.

You told Dave that you would need his preserving

bottles and jars, and that he should bring them around to your kitchen together with the fruit. Dave brought two boxes full of jars, all dusty and in need of washing and sterilising. Neither Dave nor his wife had washed them before delivering them to you. By this time, you were feeling terribly imposed upon, and you blew a gasket with Dad.

"See," you started, winding yourself up, pointing and waving your arms over the boxes, "I'm not only doing them a favour by putting in my time and ingredients (salt, vinegar, spices), but I also have to wash their bottles as well. That's where I draw the line."

Dad looked sheepishly at the bottles covered in dust and cobwebs and said nothing. He knew you were right. But he couldn't go back to the neighbour and tell him he needed to wash his own bottles, or ask him to pay for the ingredients you were putting in. No. He would have felt *virgogna*, shame.

Instead, Dad washed the bottles himself.

He never helped you when you were preserving.

That was neither the first nor the last time you had to deliver on what he had over-promised. He just never seemed to think through the consequences before committing you and your knowledge to others. He was over-generous, over-trusting, and under-cautious with some. As a result, he often got himself into fixes like this.

Other times he would simply hand over his expensive tools to people he considered friends or family and expect the tools to be returned in the condition he had lent them. Often though, the tools came back to him in unusable condition.

With those inside the family, there were times when Dad was frighteningly jealous, violent, intimidating, and abusive physically, verbally, and emotionally. In his rage he believed that you had an affair with your brother-in-law, Nino, in the mid-1950s, despite all your protests to the contrary.

Dad never forgave, nor did he ever forget.

It caused a rupture in the extended family that exists to this day. We still don't talk to that family.

It was even worse after Nino's daughter, Angela, eloped at the age of sixteen. That made her 'bad'. In fact, this was a re-run of her mother's life, your sister Antonietta, who had eloped with Nino. Double the fury...

The pressure on me to make 'right' choices, to redeem the family's honour, and to wash away its shame, increased exponentially after Angela's misadventure.

This responsibility meant also that the pressure on me to choose between your life and mine increased dramatically.

My life in exchange for yours. Sacrifice the one so the many can live on with honour.

The irony was that you never considered it unreasonable — not then, not even now, as you approach the end of your eighth decade of life.

Greater love than this hath no man that he lay down his life for his friend.

That's what I was taught in religion class. But my life was just beginning. I was just a child. How could you have expected me to sacrifice my life for yours?

170

Do what I say, don't do what I do. I got that from you, from the whole Sicilian clan, and from the Roman Catholic Church.

Your life for mine — once you're married, you can do whatever you want.

That was the promise.

Quid pro quo.

That's how you imprisoned me, with empty promises you couldn't deliver on.

Every day you lived was paid for with my life. Each day you lived, I died a little. How could you not see that? Where was the mantra that children were the most important thing in Sicilian parents' lives?

Clearly, I was the most important thing in your life, Mum, because with my sacrifice, I was keeping you alive. What about me and my life?

I had to do something, or I would take my own life.

That was the only thing I still had control over.

Then one day, when I wasn't looking, the answer

revealed itself to me: *Do what I say; don't do what I do.* Clearly, actions spoke louder than words, and what your actions were saying was that it was ok to lie, to fool others, to keep secrets, as long as you were not found out. And of course, not get pregnant in the process. That's how you got found out!

So I began plotting a way to get what I wanted without you knowing.

On the surface, I appeared to be doing what was expected of me as a teenager in the family. I kept going with you to your parents' place every Friday or Saturday night, like other Sicilian families did. Every Friday night there was often up to twenty people visiting. Poor *Nonna*. In her younger years, she seemed to enjoy having the family there.

As I got older though, *Nonna* seemed more and more burdened by this family 'joy'. It was often too much for her, but she didn't want any help. She would bring out cold drinks during summer with nuts and chips for the kids. Later, the strong, black, pungent espresso was served with cakes and biscuits she had baked, or that her children had brought to share. The three-bedroom Queenslander on stilts was always noisy at such times: the children running around the house, the women gossiping in one room, the men sitting around the dining table, smoking cigarettes and playing cards. Every now and then the women and children stopped in their tracks when one or other of the men bellowed expletives in Sicilian. When they realised he'd just received a 'bad' hand of cards, they resumed their chatting and playing.

As the oldest of the grandchildren, I was too old to play with the younger children and too young to listen in on the older women. Most of the time I didn't understand what they were talking about; mostly events that had happened in the past in the old country, people they knew from back then, plans for sewing this dress or that suit for themselves or their daughters for some occasion.

Those conversations, I think now, were very

reassuring for them but utterly boring for me. When in Sicily many years later, I saw older women sitting at their front doors, knitting and watching. They were the best-informed people in the whole village without the benefit of social media platforms. They *were* the social media.

To balance out playing the 'good' girl, the daughter you needed me to be, I needed to do something I wanted, and that always put me on a collision path with you and Dad.

In my teens, I wanted to do something completely different from what you had done as a girl. Go to parties, go dancing. Even going out alone at night would have been a big thing for me as a teenage girl. I knew that there was no way you would allow me out on my own, so I made the decision to do it anyway.

You and Dad were very afraid of the night — that was when all the crims, thieves, murderers, and rapists came out, under cover of darkness. That's the belief you passed on to me.

Fly Francesca Fly

What better way to overcome my fears, I thought, *than to face them by going out into the night on my own?*

Why would I want to do that?

I thought that if I could be unafraid of something that you and Dad were afraid of, it would make me stronger; it would mean that I shouldn't believe everything you told me. Already, I didn't believe you regarding who to trust. My experience already told me that I couldn't trust people inside the family, particularly you or Dad. You were both guilty of abuse. Not that you would have called it that, but by making your needs more important than mine when I was a child, doing whatever you had to in order to get your needs met, including using me to protect yourself, that was abuse.

I planned my exit from the house, what I was going to do once outside, and how long I would be outside for.

I chose a moonless mid-week night. I waited until everyone was asleep then crept out of bed. My heart echoed off every wall. It thundered in every footstep, rattling all the nails holding the house together.

Or so it seemed. My imagination was working overtime.

I slipped on some black pants and a long-sleeved dark skivvy and sneakers and slipped out the window of my bedroom.

At that time, we lived in the low set cottage in Spring Hill. You remember it, Mum. It had hopscotch-style casement windows with rose-pink and green frosted glass. In my bedroom, the windows opened outwards with a latch on the windowsill. Through those windows, I was able to get in and out of the house easily.

I dropped to the ground below with a thud and looked around me to see if anyone had heard. I knew that I would need a crate or a wooden fruit box to stand on to climb back in. There were always a couple lying around in the back yard waiting to be burned in the incinerator, so I knew I'd be able to get back in.

That moonless summer night, I crept out of the yard, hunched over to make myself look less visible. The only light came from dim street lamps casting long shadows. I didn't need a lot of light to see where I was going. I knew the street like the back of my hand.

As I got further away from the house, I began to walk more and more upright, but I stayed in the shadows, outside the arc of streetlights. I walked down main street to the centre, a kilometre away, and just watched from the shadows.

A few cars drove past. A police car drove past. Nothing much was happening in downtown Spring Hill. But my heart was still pounding. If I was caught, I'd be in big trouble.

Nothing happened. I saw no one except the odd drunk stumbling around on the main street after being evicted from the pub. That was where most of the action was happening. Closing time was 10 o'clock every night, Monday to Saturday. It had been changed recently from 6.00 pm to avoid the 'six o'clock swill', as it was called, when men would rush to the pub after work to get an hour's worth of beer into them before they went home. I remember Dad used to say that these men, jostling at the bar, looked like horses swilling at the trough. That sort of drinking behaviour was very foreign to him.

The great thing was that while I could see those men shuffling about on the streets, they couldn't see me hiding behind the bushes.

Arriving back home and in the safety of my bedroom, I felt a mix of satisfaction and relief.

I made a promise to myself I would do it again, and soon.

I did it a few times throughout that summer. Each time I went out, I felt my courage increase and my fears decrease. As my fears decreased, I was able to enjoy the experience more. I began to take note of houses that still had lights on after 10.00 pm. I noticed the warm humid air that hung thick with the perfume of frangipani wafting on the cool night breeze. I noticed the crickets' high-pitched chirping being loudest under streetlights, giving me away when I approached.

There was a whole world out there that I had no experience of.

After a while it was time, I thought, to go out on a Saturday night, one of the busiest nights of the week, even in Spring Hill.

The first Saturday night I went out I took the same route. By then, I knew every crack in the footpath, every tree to give me cover, every fence that could shelter me from night eyes.

I went down the back streets and, unlike every other night I'd been out, there were a lot more people around talking, laughing, making their way home, or to the next drink. There were also people sitting around in their back yards, bottles of beer close by, or in the homes of Greek and Italian migrants. They were drinking what I now know to be *ouzo* or *anisette* out of small shot glasses. In those days there weren't many restaurants in Brisbane; it was a much more sedate town than it is now.

On one such evening, I was caught out. A young man was sauntering by when he spotted me hiding in the shadows. He came over and began talking to me.

"Go away," I said, annoyed, but he lingered.

I started walking away. He followed me, and kept talking to me, asking me what I was doing.

I began to get agitated, afraid of what he might want and what he might do to get it, with or without my consent.

By this time, the blood in my veins was a sledgehammer in my temples.

Where should I go?

Now I had a choice to make: go home and lead him to where I lived or lead him somewhere else.

I walked faster and faster, ignoring him, and soon left him far behind. When I arrived home, I was very relieved.

During the following weeks, I spent hours thinking about what I had done that Saturday night and what I would do differently next time. Just thinking about doing something 'illicit' energised me. It never occurred to me that something bad would happen, even after that close encounter.

A couple of weeks later, I went out again on a Saturday night.

I went to a different spot, staying well away from streetlights, but as it turned out, he saw me again, came over and started talking to me. I didn't run away this time.

It was after the third encounter that I decided it was too risky to keep doing this. He seemed to be looking for me, which didn't sit well with me. Meeting men much older than myself (he was twenty-nine, I was sixteen) was not what I had imagined I'd be doing when I first started slipping out at night. Before things got out of hand, before anyone chanced upon what I was doing, I had to stop.

At home, I always felt on the edge of a precipice. If this ever came out, I feared I would have fallen over the edge... and I didn't know what lay there.

I stuck to the rules after that. By the time I was eighteen, and at uni, Filip would sometimes accompany me out at night. He didn't like chaperoning me and I didn't like being chaperoned. So we agreed that we would leave together and come home together, and in between we'd each do our own thing. That was how we both got to do what we wanted.

I assumed that what you didn't know wouldn't hurt you.

At university, I started attending flamenco dance classes which had only just become available. There were only a few people in the class, including a couple of young guys.

I had been drawn to flamenco since the first time I saw Rita Hayworth dance around a camp fire to gypsy guitar music in a 1960s western. The guitar music hit a chord in me, and I couldn't take my eyes off her. When flamenco became available at uni, I jumped at the opportunity.

I loved those dance classes; I loved the music, the passion, the costumes, and the pride with which the dancers held their heads and bodies: upright, proud, determined, soulful. Nothing was done by halves in flamenco. The music was full-on, the singing heartfelt, the costumes vibrant.

The dancers moved with an air of confidence, almost defiance, that said, 'This is who I am and I'm not afraid to show it.'

To a girl who was in a state of limbo about who she was, who couldn't show what she really felt, or be who she really was, this air of confidence was very seductive.

Dancing the *sevillanas* to the rhythm of the guitar music was pure joy. That's what I lived for in those days. I began going to dance classes as often as I could, and over a couple of years, I became quite good.

Anytime I was waiting at the bus stop, my feet would begin tapping. Anytime I was standing for any length of time, I would automatically take up the opening dance position with my feet. I was in love with this form of dance.

My dance teacher, Alejandra, gave me one of her skirts to practise in. It was light blue with white polka dots, fully flared, and four rows of frills. It was very heavy, just what I needed to maintain proper posture while dancing.

My performance skirts, though, were made by a local dressmaker. You used to sew at that time, but I didn't want you knowing anything about this new love of mine. I was afraid you would force me to drop it.

With the money I earned working on my days off from uni and at weekends, I had my costumes made. One that I loved was a formfitting, long, red-and-white polka-dot dress with layers of frills at the bottom. Alejandra helped me put this costume together, which included a white shawl whose ends were pinned together at the neckline with a rose. She used to travel to Spain a lot in those days, and she would bring back castanets, tortoiseshell fans, hair combs, and lacy shawls for her students when they simply weren't available anywhere else in Brisbane at the time.

Whenever I danced, I noticed out of the corner of my eye people watching me. I loved that they were spellbound. Whenever I danced I felt in the zone, like dancing on air, with the rapturous guitar music filling my ears and my body with vibrating rhythm. The music, the drama of the dance, and the power of the footwork took me to another place, a place of ecstasy. I imagined it must be the same for the whirling dervishes of Turkey. Who needed LSD or marijuana when you had this!

When I was in full costume, with my shiny black hair slicked back in a bun, a red rose in my hair, and my lips painted red, I was a different person. I felt seen and noticed, not invisible like I was at home where I felt dead and empty. Dancing made me feel alive.

When I danced, I felt beautiful.

I became so good that I began to receive invitations to perform at private parties. At first, I declined, because I knew you and Dad would never agree to my performing in public at night.

That was not how I envisaged living my life though. Once again, I called on my brother to chaperone me to those private parties. Once there, he left and returned later to pick me up.

The parties were often *juerga*, flamenco jam sessions, and they energised me immensely. There, I could forget what it was to be me in your family. There, I had wings and I could fly.

Alegrías, bulerías, fandangos... these were portals to another world for me, a world of *duende*. There were more invitations to dance, accompanied by live guitar and *cantes*, songs. All the emotion that I quashed in order to survive at home found release through this music and dance. The pain, the sadness, longing and yearning, heartbreak and despair... and joy.

I danced through the heart, and people saw that.

At one of these *juergas*, I was introduced to a special individual, a man considered an elder in the Spanish community. I had just received a personal invitation to meet him.

He had been sitting in the background enveloped in a thick cloud of cigarette smoke, watching intently.

He was probably in his 60s, I imagine. His face was square and expressionless. He wore glasses with thick lenses and had silver hair and moustache. I could see that he would have been quite a formidable figure in his youth.

What did he want?

He wanted me to dance for him personally at a private club. He offered to have a car pick me up and take me home, offering to pay me $100 for the evening.

That was quite some money back then, but I didn't jump at it. I was thinking about it when he increased it to $200. That took me by surprise, but again I didn't respond. Then he increased it to $300, which made my head turn.

I looked him straight in the eye and asked, "And what else do you want for that much money?"

"Just the pleasure of watching you dance," he replied.

Naturally, I was sceptical. What was this old man up to? I wanted some time to think before I responded.

This is going to be a one-off, and what's the harm in

doing a private show for an old man? I thought. *The money is good.* It was twice the average weekly wage for males in the 1970s. And I was being offered this amount for just one night's dancing!

I had already begun to toy with the idea of leaving home. This money could be a backup for whatever might come. It might even be the means by which I could leave home.

I didn't have to think long about it. Seeing the opportunity on offer, I agreed.

It wasn't a one-off though. He contacted me in different ways to perform for him. Each time he paid me $300 in cash. I was getting a nice nest egg together, one that I preferred you knew nothing about. I decided not to bank the money; I didn't want it showing up in my passbook. You were already in the habit of examining my passbook to check transactions and balances. The funds in this account were intended to go towards my wedding some time in the future.

That's how I survived: you were pacified knowing

that the money in my passbook was growing steadily; I got to keep the money I earned dancing for a potential rainy day which I was sure was coming.

After I had been dancing for Ignacio on and off for a few months, one evening he asked me to come over to his table after the performance. This was very unusual, but I approached his table and he asked me to sit down. I had already changed into my street clothes but was still wearing my makeup.

After a moment, he spoke. "We haven't had much chance to speak with each other. I'd like to get to know you a bit better," he commenced. I noticed again his thick Spanish accent.

"Why do you want to get to know me?" I replied cautiously. "I dance, you pay me. That's all there is to it."

"Why do you do this?" he continued.

"Do what? Dance? Dance for you? What do you mean?"

He didn't reply, and feeling my anxiety rise with the extended silence, I continued, "I love dancing, and

I like getting paid. Anything wrong with that?" I was defensive, but it was most irregular, and I didn't know where he was going with his line of questioning. Instinctively, I knew I had to be careful.

"I pay you well. What are you doing with all the money I have given you?" Ignacio asked curiously.

The question took me aback, but I replied nonchalantly, hoping to put him off. "Oh, this and that... just the usual stuff girls buy... clothes, shoes, makeup."

"You can do much more than buy those things with what I pay. What you do with the money?" he asked again, more insistently.

Suddenly I began to feel as though he knew what I planned to do, or at the very least, he knew something I didn't. I looked him straight in the eye.

"It's really none of your business what I do with the money I earn here, but if you must know, I'm saving it up to leave home."

"Girls like you don't just leave home," he replied, calmly, knowingly. "Sicilian girls don't leave home until they marry, unless..."

"Look, I have to go," I said, cutting him off. "My lift is waiting." I needed to get out of there quickly.

As I got up to leave, he called out a warning, "Stay away from Velo."

I almost ran out of the club to the car. As usual, I took my makeup off in the car while Filip drove. I didn't think any more of Ignacio or Velo, whoever he was.

Some weeks later, after a performance, I was approached by a young man dressed very smartly, too smartly and too expensively for someone so young, I thought. I was immediately wary of him. He asked me to accompany him, as someone wanted to speak to me out the back of the premises.

If I was wary before, I was on full alert now.

I demanded to know who wanted to speak to me and what about. I was told that Mr Frank Velo wanted to put a proposition to me.

That name meant nothing to me, but as he continued, Ignacio's warning slowly came back to me:

"Stay away from Velo," he had said. Could this be the same person?

The safest place was inside the premises, so I stalled for time.

"If he wants to speak to me, he should come inside," I announced, and turned to leave.

"Who do you think you are?" he spat out while looking me over from head to toe and back again, as if I were a piece of meat.

I stopped in my tracks and turned to face him.

"What Mr Velo wants, Mr Velo gets," blustered Frank Velo's mini-me.

"Yeah, well, if he wants to speak to me, it's in here," I repeated, hoping he wouldn't sense my weakening resolve.

A moment of silence followed that felt like an eternity.

The young wannabe changed his tone.

"Does your *mama* know that you dress up like this?" He spoke slowly with a sneer, barely covering the thinly-veiled threat.

"Does your *papa* know that you dance to entertain a room full of men?"

"And women..." I added hastily.

Too late I realised that the correction merely displayed the extent of my naïveté.

I thought I was street-smart, but in truth, I had all the sophistication of a twenty-year-old girl who had lived an extremely sheltered life.

I fought my natural inclination to turn away so he wouldn't see me blush, unlikely as it was under my makeup. Instinctively I knew that if I showed weakness, I was finished.

I looked up at him to see his nostrils flare. He let out a grunt and sneered.

Instantaneously and without thinking, I became the fiery Andalusian that I acted out in dance.

Tilting my head back, and with a defiant air that said, 'This is who I am and I'm not afraid to show it,' I dared him, "See if I care."

I knew I had to get out of there. The situation was deteriorating quickly.

As I whipped around to make my escape, the heavy frilled train of my performance dress jack-knifed over his shoes. Turning around one last time, I looked at his shoes, looked up at him, and with fake contriteness said, "My apologies, I didn't mean to clean your shoes." As I strutted away, he was still picking his jaw up off the floor.

Later I realised that I had picked up more than I thought from Alejandra's dance classes. I didn't have a lot, other than bluster, to help me out in such a situation.

Much later I was to learn that Velo was a Brisbane nightclub owner who was notoriously associated with drugs and illegal gambling, prostitution, and police corruption, quite common at that time in the nightclub scene in Brisbane.

Even though I didn't meet the infamous Francesco Velo that night, I knew that it wouldn't be long before he made another approach 'with a proposition'. After the release of *The Godfather* a few years earlier, the words rang in my head: "make him an offer he can't refuse". I didn't want to be in a situation where a local Sicilian, arguably involved in illicit operations, might make me an offer I couldn't refuse.

Maybe Velo was the sort of person Dad had always tried to protect all his children from. Dad had grown up on the streets during the Great Depression, in the chaos of the war and post-war years.

I knew I'd been lucky that night. Next time I wasn't sure I'd be so lucky.

Chapter 12

As I reached my dressing room to change out of my costume after the encounter with Velo's messenger, I was met by the familiar smells of stale cigarettes wrapped up with perfume and makeup. But this time, something else was happening.

I began feeling the energy seep out of my body, down my arms and out through my fingers. My arms and legs went limp, and I could barely hold myself up. The room began spinning. My heart was racing, my breathing became noticeably shallower and faster, and there was a roaring in my ears. Time slowed down and when I spoke, a part of me knew it was me speaking but strangely, it didn't feel like me. It was surreal, like it wasn't happening to me at all. The best way to describe it is I felt as if I was outside my own body, 'spaced out'.

I just had to get out of there. Suddenly this whole situation felt very dangerous and I knew I could stay no longer. I didn't know what was going to happen next.

I managed to change into my street clothes. With my head still spinning, I collected my things and left the building. To someone looking on, there was nothing unusual or different about what I was doing. In myself though, I felt I was moving in slow motion. Voices sounded as though they were coming from a vinyl record being played at a much slower speed, muffled and distorted. My head was confused, and all my movements felt like they were taking place underwater. I was fumbling with my things and couldn't get a grip on them. My words also seemed to be coming from underwater.

The anxiety had returned full blast.

I navigated my way out to my lift, but I'll never know how I made it out there. Once inside the car with Filip, I began shaking uncontrollably. As we drove off and I began to feel safe again, the shaking lessened. By the time we arrived home, my breathing had returned to normal and I was back inside myself.

It didn't stop there though.

For days and weeks after that, I couldn't think straight. Emotionally, I was up and down, and I burst into tears at the drop of a hat, or I'd get angry with little or no provocation. My grades suffered because I couldn't focus on my work. Very often I would lie in bed all curled up.

I didn't understand what was happening to me.

After that, I became unreachable. I didn't want to talk to anyone in any way associated with that part of my life. I hid away at home in the room I shared with my sister. Many days I struggled to get out of bed.

The irony is that this was all going on within me, but I couldn't let it show to the outside world—to you or anyone else in the family. 'Crazy world' rules still reigned in our family.

Despite my bravado that night, I could never be sure that Frank Velo wouldn't carry out the threats his envoy had hinted at that last night I danced.

So I did the only thing I could at that time: I stopped dancing and let Ignacio know I would not be available any more to perform for him. My studies had to come first.

When I tried to study though, I couldn't take anything in. I would read the same lines over and over, but I didn't understand what I was reading.

I couldn't put into words why I was so emotionally fragile. I just knew that I needed to feel safe. And the only place that seemed safe enough was curled up in bed with the covers over me.

I very nearly failed that semester. Any decision over and above what I was going to have for breakfast was too much for me.

I knew I was in trouble.

Emotionally, I was being pulled in many different directions. Crazy? It was schizo... various emotions seemed to be playing out and I had no control over what my mind or my body were doing. I was in crisis and I didn't know how to get out of there.

Something snapped in me that night when I felt outside of myself. It was a feeling I was to experience again and again over the next four decades, so much so that dissociating became 'normal' for me. I didn't know what it was then, nor that it was a symptom of post-traumatic stress. That term hadn't even entered the English language in the 1970s. It only became clear to me much later in life.

I was living a double life: one in the Australian society; a very different one in the home and the uprooted Sicilian community.

In the Australian society, I was told I could make my own choices of what I wanted to do with my life; at home I was told I had to stay on the straight and narrow, marry in a traditional white gown, obey my parents, and maintain the family honour and reputation.

The modern western democracy I lived in spruiked self-reliance, self-determination, and self-responsibility.

Yet within the family, your culture expected

that women rely on male authority figures who determined the lives of their women. In your culture, females assumed responsibility not for themselves and their own lives, but for their husbands, children, and extended family. This system was supported by Sicilian women themselves. This system gave women power to keep their families together, and to keep the culture alive. It was how clans had survived.

It worked for most Sicilian men and women living in small towns or villages with little or no contact with the outside world.

But for their children, born and raised in a much larger world, this small-town world view was always going to be too small.

I know that by allowing me to attend university, Dad broke a key rule of his own cultural group in relation to women. I do think now that he wanted the best for all his children, and because he himself had not had more than three years of schooling, he wanted us to take advantage of whatever educational opportunities were available to us, so we could have a better life, not one lived on the streets. In doing so, he generously and courageously opened a new pathway for the next generation, not just for his children.

At the same time, though, he expected nothing to change inside his family: he expected men to be men, as they were in the old country, and that the women, me included, would fulfil their traditional roles.

It was like being raised to stand proud and tall in the big wide world each day when I left the house to become part of the wider world, only to have to micrify myself in order to fit back into the confines of the much smaller box that was your world.

A jack-in-the-box.

The trouble with 'jack' constantly folding and unfolding is that over time, jack tears apart.

Despite all that was going on inside me, I couldn't let on that I needed help. I had learned that you couldn't handle it when I needed help. You became 'sicker' than I was. You'd throw your hands up in the air and wail.

Man, was this a sick family!

I had become frozen, unable to make decisions, unable to move in any direction.

I saw danger lurking at every turn.

I felt like a caged animal trapped in a snare.

I was getting worse. And there seemed no way out.

Chapter 13

The young couple sat on the edge of the bed in the dingy room of the men's hostel that was their first, though temporary, home together in Australia. They were grooming each other, in the way that primates do. He was running his fingers through her long, dark, thick hair, curling it around his fingers, tugging at it, gently at first, then with increasing force. Suddenly she cried out in pain.

"Stop it!" she cried. "That hurts. I don't like anyone messing with my hair."

He let go of her hair, got up off the bed, faced her, and swung his arm up and back behind him. With his open hand, he slapped her across the face, hard. He was strong—he had just spent the last two years cutting sugar cane in north Queensland.

She began to cry.

"What was that for? What have I done to you?" she asked in bewilderment.

"You've got more hair than I do," he replied coldly.

"So I should just let you pull my hair out so that you don't have to be jealous that I have more than you?" she cried in disbelief. "*Sei pazzo* (you're mad)!"

Before she could say anything else, another blow, this time with clenched fist, came down on her head. She didn't see that one coming.

He walked out of the bedroom coolly and calmly, as if nothing had happened.

Before she had a chance to collect herself from her foetal position on the bed, he called out from the next room, "*Non si mangia 'sta sera?*" (Aren't we eating tonight?)

This is how your marriage started out in Australia, you told me, and it only got worse from there, even when you were carrying his children.

Rather than punch you in the ribs or the abdomen, which would have put the baby at risk, he punched you on the head. Even your loud cries of protest and your arms flailing around your head to protect yourself didn't stop him. He was always stronger and more powerful.

As I write these words, I picture him beating you up and it makes me sad and very angry.

I have to put my pen down and walk away from my desk now for a while.

No woman should be treated like this.

Dad was always pathologically jealous of you. He imagined you doing things that made him a cuckold among his male Sicilian friends. He imagined, for example, that you were inviting the attention of the young male boarders in the boarding house. Any time you went to the city on family-related errands, he always wanted to know how long you'd been gone for, what you had done, where you'd been, who you had seen. If you were delayed, he would get insanely jealous, believing that you were doing 'business' in one of the hotels in town.

That was a disgraceful thing to accuse you of.

You didn't know him before you married him, and you didn't know what you were getting yourself into.

Yet you and your family still held to those ancient practices that prevented young men and women from getting to know each other before marriage. And when a marriage turned out like this, there was no sympathy for the woman.

'This is the hand that fate has dealt you, so just get on with it.'

That was what women in such circumstances were told by 'loving' family members: mothers, sisters, aunts.

What was the greater sin? That a young woman was at a small risk of pregnancy out of wedlock? Or that she would spend the rest of her life with a man who beat her, abused her physically, emotionally, and financially, and threatened to kill her, for the duration of their marriage?

Fathers and mothers of your generation and your parents' generation adhered to thousand-year-old practices to keep up appearances in society, but every daughter who was dispatched into such a marriage lived a life of solitary and silent desperation.

How many of these young women attempted to end their lives?

Stories whispered by the old village women told of how this woman or that had thrown herself down the communal well in the town square to end the torment.

'She was weak,' they judged, patting themselves proudly on the back while boasting of their own survival.

I heard such stories on a visit to Sicily in my adult years.

One young woman was fished out of the well and led back, sobbing hysterically, to her crying baby. The townspeople derided her, mocked her, whispered about her behind her back.

No one wanted to be associated with someone who was clearly mad. It might be contagious. They, the women, might *all* get the madness, and then where would that leave them?

She was probably suffering from what today would be diagnosed as post-natal depression. She needed help, not condemnation.

What kind of parenting could she provide her own children?

After living in Australia for twenty years, you had outgrown village life, but it suited Dad to a tee. He enjoyed going back to his hometown, spending time with his brothers, strolling down to the *piazza*, catching up with people he hadn't seen in years over a cup of espresso or a granita and cannoli, making his way back to a brother's house for lunch which his sister-in-law had been preparing all morning, and finishing off with a nap after lunch, as is the Mediterranean way. Then getting up again around three, putting on a fresh shirt, and sauntering down to the *piazza* again for another round of people-watching, espresso-drinking, card-playing, and gossiping until late. Dinner around eight, then to bed, only to do it all again the next day.

Ah, that was the life he adored! That was the life he dreamed of living when he was back in Australia working to support his family, working to achieve his dream of returning to the old country, with lots of money to splash around and yearnings of *la dolce vita*.

Hold on though. Isn't there something missing in all of this?

Where did you figure in this dream of his?

THE FAMILIES

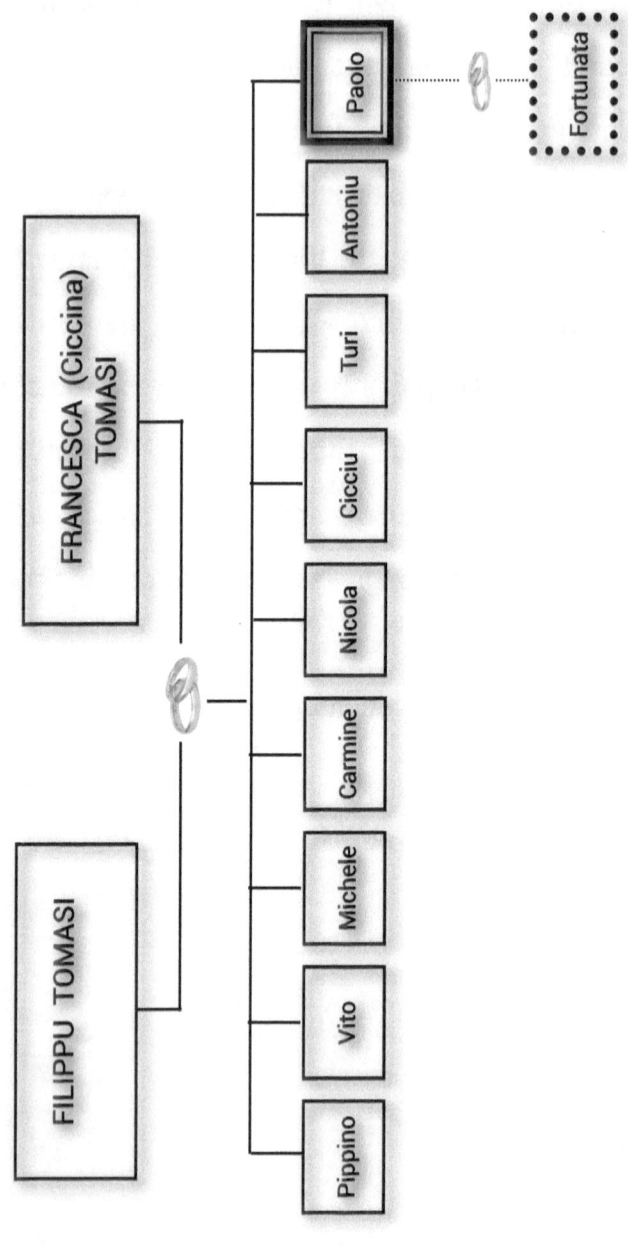

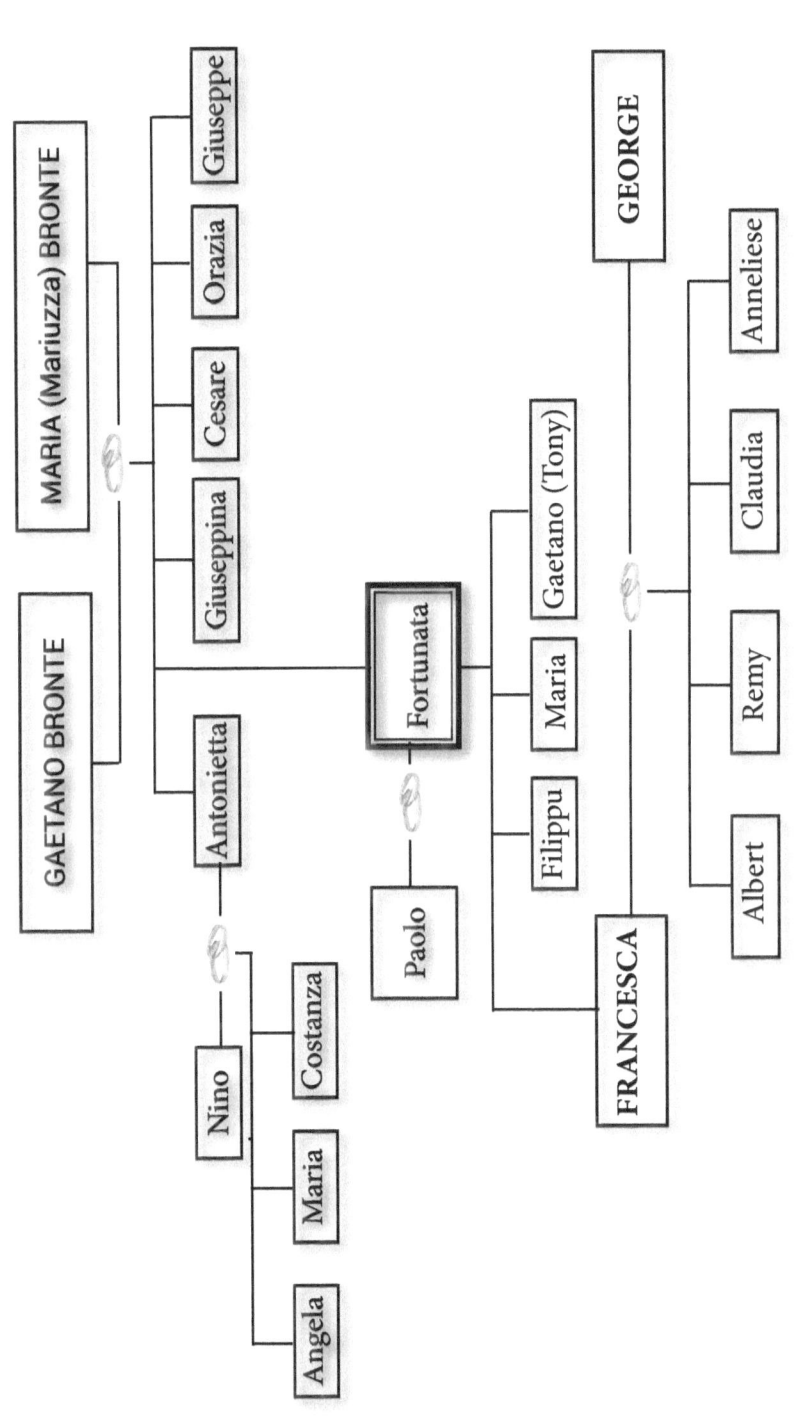

Chapter 14

"You need to go to hospital," the young doctor announced.

"What hospital? Why?" I replied.

"It's for your own good. I'm concerned you might harm yourself, or worse. And there's only one place — Warinda Park."

The name of the psychiatric hospital on the outskirts of town sent a shiver down my spine. Such institutions were never located within the city confines — the inmates might get out and go on murderous rampages through quiet suburban streets, it was believed. Or worse, the rest of society might get infected with whatever it was that ailed them. Best to keep them quarantined — for their own good, of course.

I was twenty years old, and in a doctor's surgery at the university. I had finally made the decision to get some help. I had never felt like that before. All the years before I had managed to keep a lid on my emotions, playing the part that was expected of me, keeping all I felt and thought and knew deep inside, deep in the dungeon.

But now, my defences were no longer working.

More and more, my anger was slipping through the cracks, like plumes of smoke coiling skywards, signalling imminent eruption to those who had eyes to see.

I was dissolving into tears at the drop of a hat and I didn't know why, or more importantly, how to stop it.

I was increasingly unable to account for time, sometimes seconds, sometimes longer, I never knew how long, when I was just not there. I seemed to leave my body, to dissociate from it. It happened when I was stressed or under pressure. Or simply when I had to decide between a couple of options and I couldn't, because I didn't know what you expected me to do in the situation, because I feared the consequences for either one of us if I made the 'wrong' choice.

On the merry-go-round in my head that spun faster and faster, there was no way to get off safely or to stop the spinning.

In the 1970s, most people in psychiatric hospitals were long-term chronic patients. To be told that I needed to be hospitalised in such an institution sent my anxiety levels through the roof.

"I'm not that bad that I have to go to hospital," I bargained with the doctor.

How could I tell you? What would I tell you about the reasons—that you and Dad had put me there? You had no idea then that anything was wrong. You thought my ups and downs were pretty standard for an adolescent student. Only they weren't.

As the doctor continued talking, I didn't hear a word he said.

I saw your reaction unfold in my mind. You would

throw your arms in the air in despair crying out to your God and wailing, "How could this happen? What's troubling you? If it's anything happening here at home, tell me, I'll see what I can do to help you, but you mustn't say anything to anyone... what will I tell your father?... what will my family think?... the shame... oh God... no, tell me what's troubling you, we can sort it out together... the shame... oh, the shame... no one will want to marry you... your father..."

That was when I knew that no matter how bad I felt, I had to continue the deception. I had to continue living a double life.

There must be another way... There must be another way...

The mantra reverberated through my head, pinging and ricocheting down a narrow dark tunnel that had no beginning and no end.

The cure was far worse than the illness, and it carried a price tag that was too great to pay. I would have been branded crazy for the rest of my life.

I couldn't share any of this with you at the time. I knew you couldn't cope. I was your daughter who needed help. Yet I was also your protector, confidante... your parent. I had to continue the deception that I could look after myself. And most of the time, I did. I could never, ever, bring any of my problems to you to toss them around, get a different perspective on them, or solve them. No, that was my job with you.

It wasn't just an out-of-wedlock pregnancy that could get me expelled from the family, I learned. I could also be disowned for having a mental illness, even if it happened through no fault of my own. As the first daughter, it was my responsibility to keep up a façade.

But the façade was crumbling.

The doctor wanted to put me on antidepressants.

I stared at the linoleum on the floor of his surgery, noticing uneven lines of grid tiles and black scuff marks.

I rejected the antidepressants.

What if you found them? I thought. I couldn't have you finding them—the whole façade would unravel. The antidepressants were a step too far.

"If you don't go into hospital, then at least you need to be seeing someone regularly." His voice was a distant clarion in the fog that had descended over me, permanently now.

His voice was my lifeline, my only connection to the world.

I couldn't go to hospital. You would bargain with me, plead with me for this not to happen, manipulate me with what you imagined Dad would do and say. You would use that as a lever to get me to back down, even at the expense of my health.

I was ready to throw myself down the communal well, but I knew you would only think about how others would judge you.

Having seen Dad in action many times throughout my life, I knew that he would have made a scene punctuated with lots of thunderous yelling, accusations and recriminations. He would have then walked away, his energies spent, leaving the problem for you to solve. The film ran through my mind's eye.

"*Gran' buttana*... what have you done to my daughter? How did you let this happen? No daughter of mine is going into a madhouse..."

I didn't have a lot of options. I could stay at home, or I could leave. Leaving would not solve the problem; it would only make matters worse. Where would I go? How would I live? How would I finish my studies? How would I get help for what was becoming a serious problem for me? I'd be banished from the family and get no assistance whatsoever. Was I prepared to take such a step that would change my life forever?

No, I wasn't prepared to take that step, not now while I was crashing.

I had to stay at home.

How could I stay at home?

The thoughts spun around in my head, faster and faster.

I couldn't get a grip on any of them, to somehow slow them down, to help me make a decision.

I felt myself slip outside my body again. I couldn't control it, and I didn't know how to stop it. It had become normal for me to dissociate, so when it happened it never dawned on me that it might be a symptom of something else.

Suddenly, I felt I was being sucked down a dark wormhole. I looked up into his kind eyes and pleaded for help before everything went black.

I don't know how much time passed during which I was unaware of my surrounds. The next thing I remember was a vague feeling of being pinched on the arm, and I heard his voice as if from far away.

"Francesca, Francesca, can you hear me?" he kept repeating.

As I came back into the room, I began sobbing.

For the first time in my life, there was a witness to what I was experiencing. The witness could see that I couldn't control what was happening to me. Finally, I didn't have to be completely alone in that dark prison. Someone else, some kind stranger, finally saw my suffering.

And you know what else? He showed me compassion. It soothed the pain and brought me back from the brink.

That day I had been ready to end my life.

You should have been the one to show me kindness and love. Instead, I got your emotional baggage, the family burden of responsibility for my younger siblings, your family's responsibility for their reputation, and the burden of responsibility for your life.

By then, you knew that Dad was more than just a little crazy. Instead of protecting me from that, as a mother should, you exposed me to it fully.

All the while I fantasised about being free. Free of the pain that was not my pain, free of the fear which was not my fear, free of the burdens of responsibility you dumped on me, which were also not mine.

Yet somehow, I had to navigate through these while not letting on that I was cracking under the strain of burdens that were too heavy for someone so young to bear.

Chapter 15

In 1949, in the sleepy village of Maletto, on the north-west flank of Mt Etna, nothing ever happened. The only excitement that the two young women had ever experienced had been six years before, when, during Operation Husky, hordes of American GIs had passed noisily through the region, some in jeeps, most on foot, on their way to somewhere else more important to the war effort.

On their way home from the fields that they worked with their parents, the two sisters, aged eighteen and twenty, no longer noticed the debris on the shoulders of the dirt road—the empty bottles of Coca-Cola long since inhabited by battalions of ants, the tattered paper that once harboured strips of Wrigley's chewing gum, the empty tins of GI army rations, the metal dulled by harsh summers and freezing winters.

They wandered towards home, their paltry belongings rolled up and tied to their backs. To reach their house, they had to walk through town where the men gathered after work in the *piazza*, the town square, to catch up on the local gossip, discuss work happening around town, and get paid for work completed. During the war, the *piazza* had been the place to go to share vital information about what was happening in and around town and in other villages and localities. This was where, during the war, men heard about how the war was going, the rape of women and girls in other villages by soldiers from both sides of the conflict, the massacre of the elderly, the 'liberation' of their island home by Allied Forces.

Since the young women didn't want to be seen by the townspeople after a day working in the fields – they had their pride – they took the detour around town known locally as the goat track, which they often took home. Here they passed vineyards where they helped themselves to a bunch of grapes, or a few walnuts from low-hanging branches. They were always hungry, and the countryside produced more than enough. The war had left Sicily in ruins, and there was no money for reconstruction yet. It was that time of transition when the past was still vivid in people's memories while they waited in hopeful anticipation of a brighter future.

Thin and dirty from their hard work, the sisters nevertheless would have looked attractive cleaned up and nicely dressed. Meandering along the goat track, shaped by searing lava flows from decades before, they walked carefully on the ebony basalt, oblivious to its origins. No blade of grass or swatch of green intruded on that lonely lunar landscape.

The older of the two, Antonietta, confided in her sister, Fortunata, that she liked a certain young man in town. He wanted to marry her, but their father, Gaetano, did not approve. The young man was not a good enough prospect for his daughter. He was a *carbonaro*, charcoal maker, and unlikely to have much of a future in that trade now that Sicily was on the threshold of a brand-new world. While she was disappointed, Antonietta did not go against her father's wishes. She had younger sisters who needed husbands. She knew her responsibility was to ensure they had good marriage prospects.

The two girls had been sent home from the fields early to make bread for the family. This was no simple exercise; first, they had to preheat the wood-fired oven and prepare the dough.

Antonietta sent Fortunata home to start preparing the dough while she went to fetch some kindling from the ramshackle barn where the family stored firewood and over-wintered their animals, a few hundred metres from their home.

The girls parted ways.

When Antonietta arrived at the barn, she flung the door open and stepped sure-footed into the dark-ened space, as she had many times before. Before her eyes had a chance to become accustomed to the dark, she felt someone grab her from behind and throw her onto the hay on the ground. The young man she fancied was suddenly on top of her, his hand pressing down heavily over her mouth, his familiar voice warning her against screaming. Not that there was much chance of that. His barrel chest and strong upper arms, sculpted by hormones and years of heavy lifting, ensured that her muffled cries went unheard and unanswered.

He had his way with her and when he was finished, Nino got up, buttoned himself up, and casually yet shrewdly declared, "Now we don't need your father's permission."

On arriving home, Antonietta tried to act as if nothing had happened. But it had, and she couldn't get it out of her mind. She couldn't stay under her father's roof any more. She was now 'damaged goods'. Once word got out about this, no self-respecting man would ever marry her.

She was taken in by Nino's family and after several weeks, Nino and Antonietta married, not in front of the altar in the church like other couples, but in the vestry, alone, with only Nino's mother as witness.

At least he married the whore, the locals whispered, convinced that she had led him on, or at the very least, that she had enjoyed it.

Ten years later, on the other side of the world, on a cold moonless night, a solitary cab pulled up in front of an old Queenslander. Out of the cab tumbled a lonely, dishevelled woman with a sleeping baby in her arms, holding the hand of a small child. Their figures were silhouetted against the hazy yellow light of the cab, and when the door closed, by the dim streetlight overhead. Crouched over against the cold wind, they made their way to the front door and pressed the doorbell. Time never seems to go so slowly as when waiting for relief. The little girl was shivering into her mother's hand.

"We'll be inside soon where it's warm," she soothed.

The door opened and your sister, Giuseppina, stared back at you with stunned eyes.

Taking a moment to survey the scene in front of her, Giuseppina turned to look at her three-year-old niece, then back to you holding the baby in your arms. Realising the gravity of the situation, she asked, almost in a whisper, "What are you doing here?"

"Can we come inside? The children are cold," you said.

So began the night that first time you left Dad. He had become so jealous, so violent.

"The last straw," you told Giuseppina, "was tonight. It's been really bad since Nino moved in with us. So I had to tell Paolo that Nino wouldn't leave me alone. I'd told him to leave, to go find another place to live, but he wouldn't leave, and he wouldn't leave me alone. He wanted me to sleep with him, but I couldn't do that, not to my husband, not to my children, and not to our sister, Antonietta."

The words spilled out interspersed with heavy sobs.

"Nino just wouldn't leave me alone. He hung

around the house all day instead of looking for work. Our sister, Antonietta, is back in Sicily with two young children, waiting for him to send money to buy tickets to come to Australia! And when he told me he wanted... you know... I told him that both our families would be destroyed, his and mine. It made no difference to him, he just wanted what he wanted. That was a few weeks ago. So today I told him that if he didn't leave my house of his own accord, I would have to tell my husband and he'd be thrown out onto the street. It made no difference.

"You know, we've given him a roof over his head and we've fed him till he got settled, like we did with you, so he could bring his family here. And this is how he repays me and Paolo."

"What happened tonight then?" asked Giuseppina.

Through sobs you replied: "I had to tell Paolo. I couldn't stand it any longer. Nino wouldn't leave, and he kept pestering me to be unfaithful to my husband. Of course, Paolo got mad as hell. He went down to

Nino's room, beat him up, and threw him out onto the street. I don't know where he's going to go from here. But I gave him plenty of warning and plenty of time to make other arrangements."

"After he threw Nino out of the house, Paolo came back and demanded to know what had happened between Nino and me. I told him that nothing had happened, that I had refused him outright and told him to leave. Paolo didn't believe me. He screamed at me again demanding to know what had happened."

"Then he threw me onto the bed, pulled out his *razoio* (flick knife), and threatened to slit my throat then and there. The only thing that saved me was Francesca screaming out, 'No, Papa, no!' from the doorway to the bedroom, tears streaming down her face and trembling in fear."

"Francesca is toilet-trained, but she's started wetting herself again as soon as she sees her father coming. And the baby, he starts screaming now when he just hears his voice. And when Paolo picks him up to play with him, he screams in his face. He then blames me, and demands to know what I have fed him, what I have done to make him scream at him when he picks him up. He has no idea they're afraid of him."

"Can I stay here a couple of days just till I work out what I'm going to do next?" you asked your sister and brother-in-law.

Beds were made up and the three refugees settled down to sleep. The children slept soundly, cuddled up safely with their mother, the warmth of her body a reassurance against the night's events. She, on the other hand, had a sleepless night, knowing that this was not over. This was just the beginning.

The next day, Giuseppina's husband went to visit Paolo at his workplace, and the men talked.

That night, Dad came to see you. You told me years later that I hid behind your skirts when Dad turned up. Dad bent over to pick me up, but I ran away. Then he turned to you again and demanded, "What have you done to turn my daughter against me?"

So started the evening that was supposed to bring some kind of resolution.

By the end of the evening, you had gone back to him, you told me years later.

There was nowhere else to go. There were no women's safe houses; there was no protection for women and children under the law from violent or abusive husbands. In fact, police turned a blind eye in such cases. It was generally believed that somehow the woman had brought the beatings upon herself.

The law, which was meant to protect all people in all situations and in all environments, was left at the front door of citizens' private homes. What happened behind closed doors stayed behind closed doors. Police had no mandate to interfere in marital disputes. And if alcohol was involved, men weren't held responsible for their actions.

Dad rarely drank though. But he didn't need any excuses. In his eyes, what he was doing was right, and he didn't have to justify it to anyone.

Dad was convinced that his wife had seduced Nino. And that *vigliacco* (coward) Nino, who had dishonoured his own wife back home, was now trying it on with his wife in his own home.

It seemed everyone was seducing everyone else, in his jealousy-riddled mind. Everyone was out to cuckold him. He would show everyone that he was a man, a proud honourable man, and avenge his honour, even if it meant slitting the throat of his wife.

Yes, she was the mother of his children, but were they really his children? he wondered. How could he be sure they were his? He'd seen men turn to look at his beautiful young wife. How did he know that she wasn't playing around at home while he was at work?

No, he convinced himself, something's going on here and it has to stop... one way or another.

The sound of his daughter's voice stopped him in his tracks. When he turned to look at the small child while still holding the *razoio* to his wife's throat, he saw that he would be making orphans of his children. Who would look after them? They'd end up wards of the state or worse.

He backed off his wife.

You pulled yourself free of him, terrified but relieved. You went over to pick up the child and ran out of the room. That was your first close encounter with death at my father's hands, as you've told me again and again. When you returned to him, everything went back to 'normal', as if nothing had happened. These events were never spoken of again. Nino and his family were never spoken to or of again. They were dead to our family. Except, as I grew up, I always knew there was something between the families. That family was always spoken about in hushed tones, and my grand-parents arranged family visits so that our two families never crossed paths.

Once, though, we nearly did. We arrived at my grandparents' house and they were already there. Urgent shuffling noises came from inside the house. We walked in the front door and they rushed out the back door. I caught a glimpse of your sister Antonietta's eyes bulging in terror. Dad had vowed that if Nino ever crossed his path again, that would be Nino's last day on earth.

No one dared test his resolve.

Despite all that, he didn't shirk his responsibilities as a provider for his family. In his world, he felt comfortable, worthwhile, and he understood what was going on and could control it.

Everything else in life — he just didn't understand.

He must have felt out of control, or at least out of his depth, in many situations in life.

He didn't 'get' other people, he didn't get how to make relationships or friendships work, and he didn't get how to conduct projects on his own, so he relied heavily on you to manage everything necessary to get a project off the ground. He had no patience for any of that, but when you couldn't make it work smoothly for him, he blamed you. You had to make sure everything went smoothly so as not to awaken the monster in him.

He didn't get why you insisted on going alone on projects, why you were so averse to partnerships with others. He put the blame squarely on your shoulders for being antisocial. Once or twice when you agreed to do things his way, he was forced to eat humble pie when things turned sour in the partnership he had been so keen to form. And they almost always did.

I remember you telling me about the time he joined up with his *paesano*, Pasquale, to build a house they planned to sell and split the proceeds. Dad was always scared to start projects on his own. I think he was scared of the work and the responsibility for things that he was not good at, like dealing with architects, lawyers, accountants, and banks; ordering supplies; paying invoices, hiring and paying labourers, and so on. He just wanted to work. As a result, he encouraged his partners to do all those other things that needed to be done, while he got on with laying bricks.

Over time, Pasquale proved to be a pompous *braggadoccio*, a loudmouth, bombastic and conceited. He had the gift of the gab and he bluffed his way into persuading you to hand over more and more money to the project. You had warned Dad of this before the men started down this path, but, as usual, he ignored you.

When you and Dad went to Pasquale's place one Saturday afternoon asking to see the books relating to the project, because it seemed you were putting in more money than you had expected, he refused your request and again tried to bluff his way out of it.

After you both stood your ground, Pasquale pulled out the books and there in black and white, it was clear that he was ripping you off.

Dad threatened to beat him up if he didn't remedy the situation. You told me that it didn't end well. They finished the house and sold it, but they never spoke to each other again.

You were often a better judge of character than he was. Events proved you right on this and several other occasions, but he didn't want to accept that. For him, you were either with him or against him. If you were with him, you had to agree with him on everything. The only way to have peace with him was as a silent accomplice to disastrous outcomes.

If you challenged or questioned his approach or his decisions, that meant you were against him. A proud, rigid man, it was very risky to challenge or question him. He always took it personally.

And you did challenge him. You often questioned his approach and decisions as an equal partner, and you suffered for it. Over time, the physical violence eased, but only because he saw that your judgement had been sound so many times, I imagine. Over the years, he came to mistrust you less. That's not to say that he trusted you though.

But he never stopped putting you down, he never stopped the blame game, even till his last breath.

Because he was highly sensitive, even paranoid, the climate in our family was ultra-toxic.

As a child growing up, I didn't know what was going to trigger his outbursts of rage. Was it something I did? Was it something I said? I didn't know what to do to make him stop. I couldn't control his rage, and I couldn't control the terror and anxiety that filled me and made me dissociate. The dissociation saved me. When I was in that state, I was like an animal playing dead when the predator was on the prowl.

When his rage started, there was only one place to go — underground. As with the London Blitz when the only safe place was in subway tunnels, I disappeared into the tunnels. I became invisible, saying nothing, doing nothing, hiding away for fear of either triggering him further, or worse, becoming a target.

Splitting myself into different parts was my way to survive.

Chapter 16

I don't seem to remember things from the past quite in the same way that other people do. Other people remember happy times growing up, times with their families, their friends, neighbourhood kids playing together with billy-carts and bicycles, and swimming in the local creek. They remember happy times spent with pets, holidays at the beach, family trips taken together.

But I don't.

Is that selective memory? Do they just tell such stories when in company, to turn the focus away from the bad? Maybe. But at least they have happy memories to relate.

I don't seem to have any happy memories. There must have been good, or at least less bad, times when I was growing up, but I don't recall any of them.

Most of my memories are around hurtful events, painful times, recurring nightmares for years.

I remember times when I was on high alert, scanning my environment, watching for signs of threat. And there were threats everywhere. I could never relax into the present. If it wasn't someone or something outside the family that was the threat (and it usually wasn't), then the threat came from inside. Though I never thought of it as a threat at the time. It was just what happened in our family. There were bad times, and there were less bad times. I only discovered many years later that what was happening in our family was not normal, was not the experience that most people had growing up, and it had a lot to do with why I had so little to share at school growing up.

I was different—and the other kids didn't know how to be with me.

In primary school I wore the same St Theresa's uniform they did; I drank milk at school parade, like they did; I ran and played and spoke like they did; I learned like they did, had the same homework and made the same mistakes that they did while learning. I had a mother and father and brothers and sisters, like they did. And grandparents too! But during downtime, little lunch and big lunch, they kept to themselves, and anyone who was a little different kept to themselves too.

I didn't have an anglo name like they did; I didn't have blonde hair and blue eyes, or freckles like they did; I didn't eat Vegemite or peanut butter sandwiches like they did; I didn't have the weekend experiences they did, like fishing in a tinnie, camping in the bush, going to the beach on Sundays in summer. Or even going to scouts.

No, Dad worked most weekends in the sixties, so we hardly ever went out on Sundays, as you know. Ours was not a camping, fishing, boating sort of family either. What did I have to talk about at school? The boring weekend I'd had doing my homework, studying, helping with my younger siblings, cleaning?

No one was interested in that. No one was

interested in me.

I couldn't relax, smile, laugh freely, joke, play, share myself and my differences with others. No, Aussies openly told *dagos* like us to go back where we came from.

The social environment in this country was threatening. My family environment was threatening.

And the church didn't help either. That was just as bad as anything I was experiencing. Maybe even worse. I found only moral hypocrisy in Catholic schools where sanctimonious priests and nuns taught eternal damnation and burning in the fires of purgatory if a person died in a state of sin.

No wonder I saw threats everywhere during the day, morphing into shadowy phantoms that haunted my sleep at night.

There were no environments that felt safe for me. I lived under a pall of constant threat. I had to watch myself every which way. One mistake here—I'd know about it. One mistake there—I'd get punished.

Die with a mortal sin on my soul — now that was terrifying.

What sorts of things do you think they classified as a mortal sin, Mum?

Committing murder?

Yes.

Stealing?

Yes.

Disobeying parents?

Yes.

Not attending mass on Sunday?

Yes. Even missing mass on a Sunday was a mortal sin that could send me to hell if I died without absolution.

The Catholic Church was tying me up in knots inside.

Let me tell you something I've never told you before.

In the early 1960s, when Australia became involved in the Vietnam War, I remember Sister Angela

Mary, the class teacher, telling her class of eight year olds about the yellow hordes from China who were intent on coming to take over Australia. They were working their way down through Vietnam, and they were coming to get us. They would force us to denounce our God to convert us all to something called communism. And they would do this under threat of death.

This well-intentioned but misguided Sister Angela Mary told the class that we had to resist our Chinese captors. We must not denounce God because we would be delivered to eternal damnation. If we abandoned God at the time of our trials, she informed us, God would abandon us at the time of our death.

I had nightmares afterwards about being lined up against a stone wall in front of a Chinese firing squad, my captors 'inviting' me to renounce God. In the dream I refused. Knowing what came next, I woke up every time in a lather of sweat, my heart beating a hundred miles an hour.

This was a recurring dream. The 'reds', the

communists, were well and truly under the bed of this eight-year-old.

Even as I write these words and bring up this memory, I feel twinges in my gut, anger that church officials could be permitted to frighten children as young as eight with such horror stories.

Abuse in the church and their schools was not always of a sexual nature. Much of the time it was psychological and emotional.

I learned later in life that PTSD, especially for a prolonged period, can result in memory problems and difficulty learning new things as a result of the continuous flow of stress chemicals and hormones through the body.

Fifty years counts as a prolonged period in anyone's book.

No wonder I struggle to remember things, especially happy things. Either there weren't any, or I was too focused on the threats to notice anything else.

Chapter 17

I know why the caged bird sings, ah me,
When his wing is bruised and his bosom sore,
When he beats his bars and would be free;
It is not a carol of joy or glee,
But a prayer that he sends from his heart's deep core,
But a plea, that upward to Heaven he flings –
I know why the caged bird sings.

(excerpt from *Sympathy* by P.L. Dunbar, 1872 – 1906)

I was twenty when I stopped performing at private venues, disappearing under the pretext of illness.

As I pulled myself back together, I missed dancing. I missed the way I felt when I danced.

And I was angry at myself for falling to pieces the way I had that last night I'd danced. I had seen myself as someone able to cope with anything that came my way. I had proven it, hadn't I, by not falling apart like you did every time something unexpected happened. I was strong, resilient, defiant even, and nothing was going to get the better of me. Or so I believed.

You never knew about my flamenco dancing, and I wanted to dance again, even if it was just for myself.

On one of my study days at home, in my third year at uni, I arranged for my dance partner from class, Xavier, to come over for a dance session with me. You had gone out to town, so this was a perfect opportunity.

He was twenty-two and had the smouldering good looks of the main character in the Australian movie, *Strictly Ballroom*, played by Paul Mercurio. The other girls in my flamenco class had the hots for him. But Xavier and I danced together because we were good together. When we danced we were fully in synch with each other. We danced as one.

Xavier was a friend, and I had confided a little in him about our family's culture, beliefs about honour, and my predicament in the family. But I never told him the full extent of the family secret.

When he came over, I was alone in the house, dressed in my flared and frilled polka-dot skirt, white blouse, and tap shoes.

Large enough to hold family gatherings, the family room was ideal for dancing *à deux*. While Xavier prepared the cassette, I secured the castanets on my hands. We danced and danced, and I forgot the time. As the music reached a crescendo, we finished the dance, breathing heavily in each other's arms. Looking deeply into my eyes, Xavier held me in a tight embrace, leaned over, and kissed me.

After what seemed like minutes, I heard a voice say, "What's going on here?"

"Mum?" I screamed in panic. "What are you doing here?"

The next thing I knew, you were standing behind Xavier pounding him on the back and shoulders.

"Who are you? What are you doing to my daughter?" you cried out.

Then I heard Xavier say, "Piss off, leave us alone.

Can't you see I'm dishonouring your daughter, and she's loving it!" he teased, winking at me.

Then he turned to look straight at you, and said, "That's something you can put in your prayers tonight and every night from here on."

I jumped up and as I smoothed down my dishevelled clothes, you began punching and kicking him with your pointy-toed stilettos, all the while screaming uncontrollably, "Before God, I will kill you, I will avenge my daughter's honour, and you will pay!"

Remember?

I told Xavier to leave. All the while my mind was racing. *How can I turn this around, how can I get her on my side?*

When he was gone, you and I had a little talk.

"Why?" you screamed at me. "Why did you do that? What are you wearing? Where did you get those clothes from? Why do you dishonour me and your father? After all we've done for you! What will my father and my mother say? What will the family say? How will

I tell your father? *La vergogna*, the shame... "

You just kept going on and on.

"*Stop!*" I said, loudly enough so you could hear me above your wailing. I had heard your self-pitying laments too many times over the years. In the past, they had evoked my sympathy. That day, they evoked nothing but irritation.

You suddenly stopped in your tracks, lowered your voice, and asked, "Did you sleep with him?"

"Stop and listen!" I said again, to return you to the present.

Looking me directly in the eyes, you asked, "Why, *gran' buttana*, why did you do that?"

You had already decided in your own mind what had taken place, regardless of whether it was true or not. Never let the truth get in the way of an overactive imagination!

Unable to contain myself any longer I blurted out, "Because I'm sick and tired of being afraid!"

You began pacing up and down, wringing your

hands, all the while lamenting, "What's your father going to say? What will your father do?"

The threat felt so imminent you didn't hear what I had said.

I sat down on the sofa and waited for you to take a seat beside me. You couldn't look me in the eye.

"You will not tell Dad, you will not tell *anyone*. This is our secret," I told you.

You protested. "How can I keep something like this from your father? He'll kill me if he finds out later that I betrayed him by keeping your secret. He'll throw me off the top floor of this house because I didn't protect your honour!"

"That's precisely *why* he will never know. He will never find out. You will never tell him. You will never tell your mother, your father, your sisters, or your brothers, or anyone you know. You will tell *no one!* Just like I have kept your secret all these years, now you will keep mine."

You had no solutions, just recriminations, and

as usual it was me who had to come up with a solution to the problem.

Years later, I realised that everything I'd done that day was an act of dishonour, according to your view of the world, that could have had me banished: inviting a young man to my home without your permission; being alone unchaperoned with him; dressing in costume for the dance ("You look like a whore," was how you described my appearance in my costume); dancing flamenco with a young man.

The list of 'dishonourable' things I did kept on growing.

I was just a rebel, wasn't I?

What I did learn that day was that Xavier was Ignacio's grandson. Ignacio had asked him to keep an eye on me to protect me from the likes of Frank Velo. I was very grateful for such a guardian angel. However, I had decided not to see Xavier again. I didn't need guardian angels any more. My foray into performance dancing was over.

You couldn't look me in the eye for days after that.

We argued over every little thing. You wanted to win in everything.

You opened my mail—just in case.

You monitored my phone calls, lurking in the corridor, listening in, when I was using the one and only phone in the house.

You rifled through my things and found some photographs of Xavier and me performing together. The photo that irked you the most was one in which Xavier and I were looking deeply into each other's eyes as part of the dance routine. Apparently, that was dishonourable as well.

You monitored my movements, where I was going, who I was going with, and you didn't allow me out any more of an evening even with Filip as chaperone. Most of all, you monitored my body for any signs of change that could indicate a pregnancy. Your control became total. You were highly anxious and on edge.

Some days later, Filip and Maria ripped into me.

They told me that you had tried to take an overdose of sleeping pills the night before, that you were deeply upset with me and had said there was no way out for you. You had made a dash for the sleeping pills in the cupboard, but they had stopped you from taking any.

My brother and sister then accused me of pushing you over the edge. They didn't know what was going on, but it was my fault that you had been on the verge of taking your own life.

That's when it hit me that I was completely entombed in the cage. I had no room to move, even as an adult. Whatever I did for myself would result in either Dad killing you, or you killing yourself. And if I did nothing for me, I was as good as dead too.

Of course I scoffed and told them that you were playing the martyr card.

But deep in my heart, I did not want your death on my conscience, whether by his hand or by your own.

The trap was complete.

Venera Concetta

Chapter 18

You tried to leave him several times that I know about. And there were the suicide attempts that no one ever knew about, except me.

The first time you tried to leave him was early in your marriage, over Nino. You went back to Dad, and the incident was never spoken of again.

You learned over time that that was the rule. Any disagreement or conflict between you and him was never spoken of again. And since it was never discussed, it never happened. When, at times, you did try to raise it with him, he would deny that it had ever happened, then tell you that you were crazy. He had begun gaslighting you.

The last time you walked out on him was a few

years before he died. At that stage, it didn't take much to trigger either of you. He ridiculed you for wanting to learn to drive. He knew how important that was to you, but you couldn't take the ridicule or the belittling any more.

Though you walked away from him a few times, you could never escape.

Do you have any idea how many times I tried to escape from you and everything at home over my lifetime?

I could never leave, but I was never fully there either. In the 1970s, Cat Stevens was my favourite songwriter, the song *Sad Lisa* my closest friend. He seemed to understand my anguish and loneliness. I played it over and over on my cassette player.

I moved through life in a trance-like state, touching down into reality only in the parts that demanded my most immediate attention. Study was an escape. I could focus on something real and tangible, something that could get me out of the fog.

My basic instinct was to stay safe in the family and keep my younger siblings safe. Everything else swirled around me, not touching me, not registering for me. I don't have much memory of things that happened around me. Anything associated with my safety and security, I remembered. Anything associated with my escape from there, I registered. Everything else fell by the wayside. Nothing was more important than staying safe.

In the fog, there was no lighthouse to warn of danger ahead. I had only a map in my head that was incomplete and whose parameters could, and did, reconfigure at any moment.

I could never see far enough ahead to know what danger was coming up. I could only ever see one step in front of me. At the same time, all my sensory systems were on high alert, pinging out signals to see what threats lurked around.

The threat was omnipresent.

The threat was Dad.

And there was no escape.

You were a threat for me also, yet you were also my only safe haven. You tormented me with your fears, your self-absorption, your below-the-belt criticisms of me.

You were my lighthouse, but often you led me straight onto the rocks.

I was a vessel for you, a repository for you to dump your bad feelings into.

What was I supposed to do with it all? What did you think I would do with all that crap?

I now know that you expected I would store it away, stay silent about it, and never let it emerge, entomb it in cement — my very own Chernobyl — so that it would 'disappear' for all eternity. Or simply forget it.

How could you expect me to do that when you yourself couldn't?

What did you both teach me about dealing with life, about how to get what I wanted?

Dad modelled uncontrolled rage — and he usually

got what he wanted.

You modelled limitless unburdening of your problems. Dump them onto someone else who won't betray you.

I was physically and psychologically a prisoner in this madhouse. There were no safe or socially acceptable ways for me to express what I was experiencing internally.

All that emotional garbage buried inside me was fermenting, and it was getting harder and harder for me to suppress it. I kept the lid on very firmly, but gases escaped at times. That's when I would rage at the world, at you, at him, at your customs and beliefs. One match and... *Boom!*

After the night that changed my life, I never again considered Dad someone I could feel safe with. I withdrew from him. He noticed, and he mocked me and got angry at me. I couldn't bear him looking at me, let alone touching or hugging me.

Every bit of contact was toxic — I just wanted to

vomit or cut off his head.

I couldn't stand his manic laugh.

With you, I needed the sense of safety that I thought you could give me, but you were also terrifying me at the same time.

If I came to you for help, you made out that your problems were larger and more important than mine.

Being just twelve, I came to you if I was ill or needed help. One morning, not long after that night, I told you I was feeling ill, hoping to get a sympathetic response. I wasn't prepared for what came next.

"Why do all the problems have to happen when your father's not here?" you wailed.

"*Perchè, perchè!*" why, why, you lamented, sounding frustrated and helpless.

By then, I was learning to observe people, for my survival. I knew that this was not a normal response, but I didn't expect the explosion that came that morning.

Your emotional outburst to my request for medical attention — simple enough, I thought — was like whacking a fly with a sledgehammer. I had dared to get your attention for something I thought was a necessity.

I felt as crushed as if a tonne of bricks had been dumped on me.

I couldn't know what had happened for you to react that way.

Clearly, your life was far more important than mine.

How could I even think that my problems were important enough to ask you for help?

In thick swirling eddies the fog rolled in, surrounding me, making me invisible. I let it engulf me. What else could I do?

My life, my attention, my observations all centred on staying safe. I couldn't even trust my parents. You would turn on me when I least expected, when I did something wrong, when I did nothing wrong, when I did nothing at all, when I needed help.

I watched and waited from inside the foggy cocoon that had begun to entomb me.

Were you in a good mood or a bad mood?

Were you laughing or crying, angry or relaxed?

Even when you were laughing that was no guarantee you were happy.

Your laughter was often hysterical, bordering on manic.

How could a twelve-year-old child tell the difference?

How could a twelve-year-old child know when, or even if, it was safe to approach her mother with a medical problem?

I couldn't. The map had changed again, to suit you.

I just stopped telling you anything about me. I wound the silken filament tighter and tighter around myself to seal my cocoon hermetically. I figured that if I was wound up tightly enough, no one would be able to see me, touch me, or hurt me. Curled up inside the cocoon, I thought I'd be safe from the awfulness that came at me.

There was no cocoon strong enough or thick enough to keep me safe though. I bled inside the cocoon.

And no one noticed.

No one knew.

And there was no one I could turn to for help.

I had dreams, and they helped.

Dreams were full of hope, but they were just that — dreams. I could dream on, but every day the challenge in my reality was to stay safe. I did it by not prodding the predator or waking the tiger; I stayed under the radar, not attracting attention to myself, plotting and planning and dreaming, as long as you knew nothing of it. And even when I told you I wanted to leave home around the age of nineteen, you begged and pleaded with me not to leave.

So I put that plan on the backburner and continued fantasising about my escape.

My only means of escape was marriage. But since you closed off all possibilities of my meeting anyone socially, marriage seemed as likely an escape route as man landing on Mars.

I endured more than ten years of living like this, day in day out, vigilant all the time, with unabated stress from you and him, as well as from the increasingly higher levels of study. A sense of impending doom was my constant companion. I was completely at the mercy of parents who were unpredictable, explosive, and mentally and emotionally unstable.

How could I move forward in my life?

I would take one step forward, and freeze. Another step, then freeze. Most of the time I tended to go around in circles within the confines of my cage, flapping against the bars, trying to get out.

When it came to doing anything for myself or for my career, it was like being in that fog again. I couldn't seem to see beyond my feet. Going out into the world outside the cage was terrifying for me.

In my adolescent years, and since, I became obsessed with the need to know what was around the corner, knowing what threats, risks, or dangers were up ahead. I couldn't see them. I didn't know what they were or where they were. I didn't know how to prepare for them or how to protect myself from them. I stressed about this a lot, on top of everything else I stressed about. How could I keep myself safe when I didn't know who or what was a possible threat, when it could come, or in what form?

It was around the age of thirteen that I had a nightmare that recurred over many years.

In the distance was a mountain, a single volcanic peak rising from arid plains. The sky always appeared in splotchy shades of blood-red. The scene was dark with a sense of foreboding.

In this dream, you were running frantically along a road winding up and around the mountain, always upwards towards the peak, and I was following you, running frantically. From a long-distance perspective, I saw that we were being pursued by a giant cockroach. We both looked like ants in comparison. The behemoth was running on its hind legs, making it look even more sinister.

Up the mountain we ran until we reached the top, then down the mountain again, around and around to the plains. Then we'd start all over again, up and around, then down and around again.

I used to wake up in a sweat, terrified by this nightmare. The cockroach was never far behind. It kept pace with us, but never caught us. I was always just one step ahead of it. But it never ever let up.

I couldn't tell anyone about this dream. Who was there to tell? Who would listen without mocking or condemnation?

It recurred over about five years. I became afraid to go to sleep.

One night during this nightmare, I decided to do something different. Every time until then, the dream had finished the same.

This time, I stopped in my tracks and turned to face the cockroach.

Suddenly, the cockroach was just a normal size and I could step on it. And that's exactly what I did.

The nightmare never came back. Turning to face the fear eliminated it.

But in that nightmare, you continued running, never turning to look back.

Chapter 19

Over my lifetime, I have been ill three times due to stress. The first time I was just twelve.

I wasn't allowed to show any signs of distress or neediness, nor could I let you know I was struggling after that night. So my body took over to protect itself.

When the issue had been settled for everyone else, I fell ill with a condition that lingered for weeks despite medication.

I was sent to a paediatrician who determined that what was wrong with me was not physical, but rather psychological, and he recommended seeing a child psychiatrist.

When we arrived home, you gave me a long speech, wailing about the shame of having a child who was defective, the stigma associated with seeing a psychiatrist and how that would affect my life and the lives of my brothers and sister, the whole family. Oh, and, if there was anything bothering me, you said I should tell only you. We don't wash our dirty linen in public.

That was your idea of a pep talk.

Well, I never did see the psychiatrist, you might remember. I was better within a week.

What happened?

Your pep talk worked. I complied with your demands because I needed you, as any twelve-year-old daughter needs her mother.

On reflection many years later, I understood why the illness had lingered. When I was ill, I noticed that you and Dad didn't fight. There was peace in the house, and you cared for me in a way you never did when I was well. I needed loving kindness, and it seems that a part of me realised the only way to get it was to be ill.

Of course, as soon as I recovered, the loving kindness stopped, and the pressure was on again.

The second time I became ill was at the age of twenty, with a double whammy: the threat from Velo's messenger and you finding me with Xavier.

Even though you and I had a pact of secrecy over my dancing with Xavier, I never trusted you. You never knew how stressed I was, nor did I ever let on how ill I was.

Do you know why I kept it from you? Because I knew you would immediately turn the tables on me and impress on me how much sicker you were than me.

Then came New Year's Eve after my twentieth birthday.

Dad had promised to take the family to the Italian Club for the New Year's Eve dance. Now, I didn't particularly care to go to the Italian Club, but it was the only thing on offer. It was better than staying at home.

Do you remember how things worked at the Italian Club? Unless you went often, or you went with your own partner, the chances of a girl being invited onto the dance floor were remote. Girls were expected to sit quietly, like wallflowers, with their parents, waiting until a young adventurer came over and asked her to dance. She might have one dance with the stranger, maybe a couple, then she was escorted back to her table, to her parents. While she was on the dance floor, her mother never took her eyes off her daughter, in case he held her too tightly, or he tried to steal a kiss, or they left to go outside alone.

All forbidden acts.

Even an evening of this was better than staying at home on NYE at the ripe old age of twenty.

I just wanted to get out of the hell-hole for a few hours.

If a Sicilian girl wasn't married by the time she was twenty-one, people believed that there must be some-thing wrong with her, so she wasn't worth pursuing. She was already an old spinster.

When the time came and I reminded Dad of his promise to take the family to the Italian Club, he laughed scornfully, telling me that I was mad, that I was making it up, and that he had never said anything of the sort.

"Go to bed!" he bellowed, dismissing me with the imperiousness of Caesar.

I looked to you for support but received none.

I don't know what I thought you could do about it. Often you could turn him around, but on this occasion, you did nothing.

So there I was, twenty years of age, sitting at home on New Year's Eve, alone, having believed for some time that I'd finally be going to the party. No family event, no friends to invite me somewhere, no dancing, no music, no joy... nothing but emptiness and tears.

And rage.

The irony was that thirty years later, I would go to a New Year's Eve party on the day of his funeral... *In your face!*

Rage often overtook me after that.

Rage at the injustice — he was an adult who was supposed to be a role model for me and the younger children. What was he role-modelling? How to get out of doing what he didn't want to do, how to lie his way out of a commitment; how to gaslight his own children?

What set of double standards did this man live by to say to his daughter, 'make one mistake and you'll be kicked out', while many of the things he did were considered unacceptable by society in general and Sicilian society in particular?

But that was ok for him — he was the law in our house. And the law changed according to how the law was feeling, not according to what was right or wrong.

He was slippery and unpredictable, and emotionally, he was a child with far too much power and far too little maturity. I know that now.

Several months after you discovered me with Xavier, Dad's refusal to take us to the New Year's Eve dance was the last straw, proving to me once and for all that there was no way out of the prison.

My world came crashing down around me early the following year, and the doctor at the university medical clinic referred me to the psychiatrist on campus after I refused to be hospitalised.

After weeks of attending counselling sessions at uni, I began to see a way through the minefield that was my life.

While I was looking for some stability, working out who I was, what I believed in and what I stood for, I decided that I would be what he was not.

Where his behaviour was fickle and lacked consistency, I told myself I would be consistent, even if it hurt me.

Where he lacked integrity, I would display integrity in my decisions and actions. I would be ethical and honest in my dealings with others.

Where he slithered to get out of commitments he had made, I would fulfil my commitments, and where necessary, stand and face the music.

Where he raged, threatened, assaulted, and intimidated to get what he wanted, I would discuss, negotiate, compromise.

Where he threatened others to extricate himself

from tight spots of his own making, I would take responsibility for the consequences of my actions and look for ways to get out of such situations legitimately and appropriately.

Where his unpredictability terrorised those in his care, I would learn ways to lend certainty and stability for myself and others.

That was the beginning of my alternative way of being in the world. The mantra I had repeated so many times over so many years was now coming into being.

There must be another way was evolving into *there is another way*.

The girl lost in the fog was beginning to see a way through.

But I was still avoiding the most important issue. The psychiatrist wouldn't let it go because it was the root cause of all my distress, the core of the boil.

It became clear to me that there was only one way I could live my life the way I chose, and that was to simply take my freedom and leave home.

You told me many times over the years that you had left him three times, but you hadn't really. If you had been serious about leaving him, you would have done it differently. You had no plan of where to go, what to do, where to live, how to get your belongings. You had nothing in place to support yourself when you left.

And that's probably why the 'law' spared your life.

With me though, it was different.

The psychiatrist told me that there was only one way out of the cage — I had to leave home.

I remember that session as if it were yesterday.

I sat there in that room that smelled of musty books and dust. I looked at him, then stared down at the worn grey vinyl tiles. I knew he was right.

The silence in the room was broken only by cicadas and birdsong in the trees outside his window. As I retreated further into my own world of thoughts, even those sounds faded away.

I know I have to leave...

If you do, he'll never let you back in the house... you'll

283

be banished forever.

I can't keep living like this...

He'll kill Mum, or beat her up if I leave...

I'm going insane living like this with parents who are hell-bent on destroying each other and me...

Oh the shame, the shame I'll have to live with...

On and on it went in my head like this.

I sat there looking at my feet, not saying anything, not giving anything away of the turmoil that was going on inside my head and my gut.

How can I leave Mum? She'll be completely at his mercy.

Many years later, I realised I was experiencing my very own Stockholm Syndrome in that room.

I was torn in two. This was the most gut-wrenching decision I had ever had to make to that point in my life.

I knew that if I evaded the decision, or put it off for another day, this therapist would not be able to help me any further.

There was only one way out.

They're just going to let you walk out, are they? the voice inside my head challenged.

I imagined you swallowing sleeping pills to end your life. I imagined you pleading with me not to leave. I saw him rage at you, and at me, his 'ungrateful' daughter. I imagined the atmosphere in the house, tense, terrifying...

Stop! No more!

The words resounded in my head.

Why is it up to me to have to make this decision, I pleaded with nobody there.

The answer came back immediately inside my head: *because they can't and won't make any decisions to make their lives different, so you have to make the decision to make your life different.*

They can't make that decision for you.

Here I was, age twenty, at the end of myself, having to make a decision which I'd been told repeatedly for years would result in exile, expelled forever, shamed and humiliated.

I decided in favour of my sanity, of my well-being, of my life, even though it meant that there could be consequences the likes of which I had never till then experienced.

I made the decision to leave home, even though other Sicilian girls and young women stayed at home until they were married, as was customary, so the family would not be shamed.

I was dead if I stayed, and dead if I left.

Embracing the inevitable, I looked up from the floor. "Yes, I know I have to leave. I've decided—I'm leaving home."

In making this decision, I put my health and well-being ahead of everything else.

Then a strange thing happened.

The swirling gut-wrenching emotions that were wringing all life out of me stopped. An incredible peace came over me as I surrendered. I smiled and wiped the tears from my eyes and felt free, free of the terror I'd lived with for much of my life. It was a lightness of being I'd never experienced before.

This must be what joy feels like, I thought.

As well as feeling differently, I now had a new focus for my life, and I became single-minded about it. This was my final year at university and I would use the coming months to prepare my departure. I was now starting to feel euphoric, but the psychiatrist warned me that, like every single aspect of my life up until then, I had to make my preparations in secret so that you would find out about it only after all the pieces were in place.

I even used his work address to receive responses to interstate job applications. Why?

Well, you opened all my mail, of course, even after I had turned twenty-one, despite my protests.

"I have to know what's going on here," you would say to justify your actions.

Now I understand why you did what you did: the intrusions into my privacy, your confiscating my bank book (yes, even at twenty-one), keeping me on a short leash, controlling. It was all so you wouldn't get any nasty surprises, to save yourself from further attacks from the 'law'. I get that now. But back then, I couldn't let you even suspect what I was up to for fear that you would try to stop me.

Maybe you couldn't save yourself, but I was certainly going to save myself.

I had to get out of there.

And I had to plan it carefully.

One day, when I wasn't even looking or thinking or feeling, just being present in the moment, alone in my room, it happened. An experience so joyful that I felt I was seeing the world for the first time.

After years of being in a very dark place, where I had to hide what I was going through, who I was, what I felt, what I thought, what problems I had, while carrying you and the belief that your life depended on my decisions and actions, full of rage at the injustice of my situation, suddenly my eyes were open and I saw the world as if from a mountaintop—crystal-clear, bright sharp colours, and oh so full of joy!

I was smiling from ear to ear, and nothing could wipe the smile off my face.

I figured this must be the experience that the Catholic saints had when they wrote about ecstasy and oneness with God. I felt no fear, a new experience for me. This was the freedom I had been seeking! Freedom from fear!

For days and weeks and months after that, I stayed in the moment, in the now, in that space of joy, working on my studies, planning my exit.

Everything that was happening at home was just water off a duck's back. I didn't get involved, I was left alone with my work, and I continued feeling ecstatic. But I had to tone down even this feeling while at home so as not to arouse suspicion.

What drugs was I using? I imagined you might ask.

I took no drugs. The psychiatrist recommended I take Valium to help calm me down during the worst of it, but I refused.

"Drugs only dull the pain," I told him, "they don't solve the problems. And I want to have full control of my faculties to solve my problems... quite apart from the fact that my mother will find the drugs and demand to know what they are. The less she knows the better," I told him.

It was after this experience of joy that things began to change for me. New hope emerged from the depths of despair; where previously there had been darkness now shone the biggest brightest light I could never have imagined.

Not only did my studies become easier for me, but I also seemed to attract people who, previously, would not have been interested in striking up a relationship with me.

One of those people was the man who is now my husband. One of the most fascinating things about feeling such joy was that I began to feel that I no longer needed to be rescued from the family. I had choices and options open to me. I could leave home when I graduated, and get a job in another state, or I could stay at home. And that was so liberating.

When I met George, I didn't need a knight in shining armour to rescue me from the fortress which was your home. I was able to relax and be myself, and that was clearly very attractive to a man who had just spent three months living in a Buddhist monastery high up in the mountains of Ladakh.

Chapter 20

Our courtship was very strange indeed.

We met at a dinner party that a friend arranged. I was already twenty-one, that age when a child becomes an adult, or so I was told.

After months of forbidding me to go out at night with Filip, you began to ease up a little. I guess you were convinced that nothing had happened between me and Xavier that last time we danced together.

Filip and I renewed our arrangement; he dropped me off and picked me up at the end of the evening and we came home together. Nothing had changed simply because I had come of age.

That night, I met a wonderful man. We talked all night, and I felt like I'd known him all my life. I had never met anyone like that before. Sure, I'd met a lot of people at uni, but he was different. There was an astuteness about him that gave the sense that he'd been around. And he had. He had travelled east from central Europe, through the Middle East, Turkey and Persia, through the deserts of Central Asia and Afghanistan, and had stayed in the Orient for some time. Exotic placenames like Casablanca, Istanbul, Damascus, Tehran, Persepolis, Kabul, Ladakh, Burma, rolled easily off his tongue.

He had studied the Koran and learned some Turkish and Arab customs to show respect for people through whose countries he was travelling, where even a small knowledge of the local language could mean the difference between life and death.

He had dined around open campfires with desert nomads, and drunk copious cups of *chai* in bazaars in Isfahan while bartering for days to purchase the Persian rug he had his eye on.

He had studied with Buddhist monks high up in the mountains of Ladakh for three months.

There was no doubt he was unusual. There was a serenity and a presence about him that I had never sensed in anyone else.

We met a few times after that night, at uni, where it was safe for us to meet. He fit in to the student scene very well. At the time we all had either big hair Afro style, or long hair. I had the Afro, he had the long hair.

This was a friendship like no other; still I didn't give a second thought to what was developing between us. I was making my own plans to leave home. I'd been offered a contract to teach English at a high school in Arles in the south of France, and George was just passing through. We would never see each other again. So of course I didn't think of a future with him.

Those were the best days of my life to that point.

We had lunch together on the green at the university, and within a few weeks, the friendship had deepened into something else.

Then he asked me to marry him.

Without a second thought, I said, "Yes."

And with that came the awful churning in my gut that was so familiar, that falling spiralling sensation that I had not experienced in a while.

How will I tell my parents?

What will they think of me marrying this long-haired bearded guy who's just spent months up in the Himalayas navel-gazing and not holding down a proper job?

How is this 'courtship' going to move forward under the watchful eyes of the family?

My heart sank as these thoughts began circling around in my head, like sharks.

Being a tourist, he was required to leave the country and apply for residence status from his home country. He was prepared to cut his own trip short to marry me and take me away with him. He was just halfway through his round-the-world trip.

I didn't know how to feel about that. No one had ever done anything like that for me before.

No one had ever shown me the kind of selfless love that he was now showing me. I was overjoyed. And it felt right.

Once he'd adjusted his plans, it was time to bring him home and introduce him to you.

George wore his best travelling clothes. He sported a full, black beard that reached halfway to his waist, and a handlebar moustache.

He was so different from anyone you or Dad had ever encountered before. And I didn't expect it to go well.

But he was the mirror reflection of the real me inside – a rebel through and through.

When he came to meet you the first time, I led him into the lounge, the formal area of the house reserved for first-time visitors. The idea of such a room was to give a good impression of the family before they were permitted to enter the inner sanctum of the house: the kitchen and family living area.

You were very proud of your lounge, tastefully decorated in cream coloured wallpaper and enhanced by the Italian baroque lounge suite in cream and rose pink velvet. That lounge suite represented your pride and hard work. For me it was another brick in the façade, another possession to measure your progress with. Those you had used along the way were buried under that lounge, stuck behind the wallpaper, the voices of innocence silenced and papered over.

I didn't give a shit about it. It was your symbol of success, not mine.

So there we were, sitting on the Italian lounge suite, the four of us.

You were nervous, maybe with good reason.

I was nervous. I didn't know how this was going to turn out.

Knowing Dad's violent temper and his unpredict-ability, I didn't know whether he would turn George out onto the street, or throw him over the balcony to the ground below, three storeys down.

I knew one thing though: no matter what Dad said or did, I was standing by George, and I was prepared to leave home if Dad created trouble.

What I saw that evening surprised me, and I

think you too.

Dad was controlled.

Even though he had always condemned long-haired louts and had yelled at the television screen when he'd seen them protesting on the streets against the war in Vietnam, he was polite to George.

And George, of course, was serene, self-contained, knowing.

He had met many Sicilians. Many had gone north to live in Central European countries as guest workers in the 1950s and '60s. He knew the history of the island and its people. He knew of the Arab influence on the culture. He knew he was dealing with people for whom honour and 'face' were more important than life itself. He knew that these people would kill to avenge their or their family's honour, if it was compromised. By desiring a daughter of this culture, he knew he was putting his own life at risk.

But only if he broke the rules.

Then Dad started laying down the law.

I just shook my head as I heard him talk. The old beliefs about honour and 'face' and shame.

So what were the rules, according to the law?

Dad told George, in a very cavalier manner, that he should go back home and get his papers sorted out, and when he came back, he could start courting me. He would not allow an engagement to take place before George left. What if he didn't come back at all?

George did not meet Dad's idea of an ideal husband for me, did he? He was so... different, and of course, he was from north of the Alps. He was not going to be betrayed by a former World War II ally, overlooking entirely the fact that it was Italy that had betrayed the Axis. But let's not get bogged down in minor historical facts.

Even thirty years after the end of the war, he was still holding a grudge against former allies. Why? Again, I just shook my head in disbelief. He valued history as a tool for decision-making over what would make me happy.

What a surprise!

I couldn't respect him any less because I had no respect for him by that stage. I didn't disrespect him though either. I just avoided him.

Even before George came to the house to meet you and Dad, I already had some idea of the obstacles I was going to encounter from your side. I needed to know what sort of challenges I could expect in future, from both sides, so I asked George what he thought of you both.

As it was, you met his expectations of Sicilian parents: he saw you as typical of most Catholic Sicilians. With his knowledge of Sicily, its history, customs and people, he certainly did not come to your house that night with a fanciful request or unrealistic expectations. He was serious, and he wanted you to know that. The fact that Dad left the door open to an engagement on George's return was a positive outcome, he thought. But, as he told me some time later, he would have come back for me come hell or high water, and he would have taken me away with or without Dad's consent.

He came that night, ready for anything, Mum, even for a fight.

Ultimately, George wanted to take me out of our nuclear and extended family, even out of Brisbane. He wanted me to have an experience of a different world, a different family, an alternative life.

Later in life, I found conversations between Dad and George very interesting. Dad would often make many historically inaccurate statements, but history was a subject that George was well versed in. And George would correct Dad, but in such a way that he didn't lose face.

George returned to his home in Austria, and he was away for six months until his residency paperwork was finalised. In that whole time, Dad never once uttered his name. He never once asked if George ever wrote to me.

It was as if the meeting had never taken place.

Chapter 21

Then one day, George was back.

You were nervous. I was even more nervous than you.

What was going to happen? How would Dad react? What would he say? What would he do?

There were many awkward moments when Dad came home from work; many moments filled with silence and dread. Dad didn't talk, so you never really knew what he was thinking. He was unpredictable, an unknown and unknowable quantity. You had become pretty good at reading him over the years, but this was new, unchartered territory.

I was on tenterhooks. The hypervigilance was back in full force. I was constantly scanning around me, watching him, watching you, watching you watch him... Be prepared. The all-too-familiar fogginess began to return.

Dad acknowledged George, followed by small talk. And then George opened the discussion.

"You know why I'm back here, Paolo."

"We'll talk after dinner," Dad replied. He didn't want to get started on an empty stomach.

We all ate in silence, grateful for the background noise of the nightly television news.

After dinner, the two men moved to the lounge, leaving the women and children to sort out the washing up.

Dad told George the rules: during the courtship, he could come and see me at home and at family functions, but we would not be allowed out alone together. That was it. It was over in a matter of minutes.

George had been prepared to island-hop his way back if the bureaucracy had taken much longer. Even on his way back to Austria he had had major obstacles to overcome. I only found out about these after he came back.

He had taken a flight from Brisbane to Singapore where he bought a flight to Vienna via Moscow on Aeroflot, the national airline of the former Soviet Union. En route to Moscow, the flight stopped in New Delhi and Tashkent on the ancient Silk Road. Once in Moscow, all passengers were required to disembark from the plane and board a bus. They were taken to a hotel in the centre of Moscow where passports were confiscated. They were held there for three days without explanation.

Many passengers protested. They were rude to their hosts, complained about the food, and demanded to know when they would be released to continue their journey. They were particularly angry that they were not allowed any contact with their respective embassies.

Observing the other passengers, George decided on a different approach. He was already widely travelled. He knew the way to get through this was with calm acceptance and respect. He was right. Courtesy won out in the end. Passengers who were gracious to their hosts were offered sandwiches and vodka, the others were offered bread and water.

To discourage the 'guests' from leaving the hotel and embarking on unescorted tours of Moscow, armed guards were stationed at the lifts and at the entrance to the hotel.

Eventually, they enjoyed Russian hospitality during guided tours, hospitality generously offered them as long as they remained under guard in the group.

After three days, all the passengers from that flight were escorted back to the airport where they were allowed to resume their journey. On arrival in Vienna, they were taken aside by the country's border police and questioned about their experience in Moscow.

Remember, this was still the time of the Cold War.

After such experiences, he returned to the micro-cosm of Brisbane to have Sicilian law proclaimed to him. Again he decided that calm acceptance and respect was called for.

What you never knew though is that he had asked me to elope with him, to get around the silly rituals and customs around courtship. And I had refused.

I knew that if I eloped, I would be alienated from the family for a long time, if not for all time, and Dad would take his anger out on you. I knew that I couldn't be happy knowing that my happiness had been bought at your expense, possibly even at the expense of your life.

Such was the noose that you — and he — had placed around my neck.

The only way to get free of the noose was to play the game by your rules.

I thought I knew what the rules were, but I was to find out very soon that another minefield was to open up for which I had no map or directions.

Sure, there was the one cardinal rule: not allowed out alone together, even though I was twenty-two. At my twenty-first birthday party Dad had told the guests that he was giving me the keys to adulthood and I was responsible for my own choices and decisions.

So, I could make my own decisions as an adult, but I couldn't make the decision to go out with my fiancé, also a responsible adult.

I'd never been in this situation before and I had no idea what to expect.

We decided on a date for the wedding, and the courtship began.

Chapter 22

When George left that first evening, I showed him to the front door. As we were saying our goodbyes, grateful to have a moment alone together, George told me that he had come back only for me, to get me out of that golden cage as he called it. It was a moment full of promise. I looked into his eyes and felt a rekindling of the warmth and freedom I had known with him before he had gone away.

Then came the clatter of glass on glass, signalling your appearance. The moment evaporated as if in a puff of smoke.

You had come to put the milk bottles out for the milkman the next morning, as usual.

You smiled knowingly. After putting the milk

bottles on the ground, you straightened up, folded your arms, and there you stayed.

We waited expectantly for you to go back inside.

You waited with us.

After a few awkward seconds, it became clear that you were not going to leave us alone. God forbid, he might steal a kiss from me!

George said goodnight turned and left.

I went straight to bed, fuming. I couldn't discuss this with you then — there were too many ears around to hear. I waited until the next morning.

"What was that about last night?" I asked you.

"What?" you replied.

"With the milk bottles? And then staying on until he left?"

"What do you expect? That I leave you alone out there with him? He could give you a kiss."

"So?" I replied. "What's wrong with that? We're both adults."

"When your father was courting me," you

continued, "I was never alone with him."

"That was thirty years ago!" I cried. "Things have moved on since then."

"Not in our family they haven't," you announced.

And that was that. From then on, I knew there would be two courtships for my marriage: one for *l'occhio sociale*, Sicilian society's eyes, and a secret one, just for us. We could not be ourselves in the presence of my family.

I would have to split myself off in two again. In your presence and Dad's, I would be formal with George, not show any emotion, vulnerability, humanness, or affection.

In secret, I could be myself. George seemed to know this, and he played along.

He came over to the house a few nights a week to see me, but we were never alone together. Either you sat with us, or Filip did. When we escaped outside onto the balcony, two minutes later you were there. Dad, as usual, would eat dinner and fall asleep in front of the TV, leaving the responsibility of looking out for the family honour squarely on your shoulders.

At the end of each visit, you would come outside and put the milk bottles out.

After the first time, we made a joke of it. We three knew what was going on, and George used to tease you gently about it for many years afterwards.

Years later, George told me of a conversation he'd had with Dad not long after he came back. George told Dad that he hadn't come back for him or for you. He had come back just for me. George looked Dad straight in the eye and told him, "This is not to diminish you or your wife, but Francesca is my focus." Dad responded with a scowl, but George just continued looking at him.

As George told me years later, in that moment, he knew that if he slipped up, Dad would kill him. But equally, Dad seemed to know that if he interfered in this marriage, George would come after him as well.

The two men had sized each other up early in the courtship.

To conduct our secret courtship, we met in the grounds of the university where I worked. He lived close to campus, so at times I would sneak away to meet him for lunch. But I had to drive past a site on the main road to the university where Dad was working. To avoid being seen, I had George crouch in the back of the car till we had passed the site.

Other times, George visited me in my office so we could spend some time alone without parents or children watching.

So, yes, we did get around your rules. We were adults. I was an adult. Dad had said this to family and friends at my twenty-first birthday, saying I could make my own decisions. So I did.

Still though, I felt like I was doing something very wrong, very underhanded, in the Sicilian view of things.

How could I marry someone I didn't know well enough? I asked you.

You had no answers either. Nothing in your upbringing had prepared you for the questions I was asking. You never even asked such questions, you told me.

Family honour must be preserved at all costs. I thought I understood what that meant: I should not have a child out of wedlock; I should not marry someone without the blessing of the head of the family.

I was the second female to get married in this new generation. My cousin Angela, in rebellion, had eloped at sixteen and married against her parents' wishes.

But you and Dad were going to get it right, *basta*.

You set down the rules and made me accountable not just for your honour, but for the honour of the entire clan.

You are different from Angela, you told me. We are different from that family.

Your parents also pressured you to make sure that I didn't elope, that I married with the peace and blessing of the whole family.

For Dad, it was more than his honour at stake. If I had eloped, if I had done what Angela had done, it would have made him look no better than her father Nino, whom Dad had thrown out of your house twenty years before. Dad was different, wasn't he? Dad was a man of honour, wasn't he?

That was how he saw himself.

You implored me to remain chaste. You tried motivating me to do so by telling me that I would receive very nice gifts if I married with the accord of the whole family.

You threatened to take an overdose if I stepped outside of the 'boot'.

And finally, you told me that you feared for your life if I didn't comply.

That was the only argument that made me endure the next few months of this schizo living.

Easter was just around the corner after George returned.

There were always family gatherings for that. While some observed the Lenten period leading up to

Easter Sunday, in our family, the only sign that this was a time of self-denial was fish dinners on Friday nights.

I had stopped attending Sunday mass—I didn't believe any more. I had lost confidence in the church and its representatives. The church after all was an organisation that had all the strengths and weaknesses of a male-dominated hierarchical organisation. I'd had enough of them, even as they continued pointing out to the brethren that they should work harder on themselves to be the children of God that God expected them to be. The church was just like my own home dynamics—do as we say, not what we do.

Who were they kidding?

You and I had conversations about religion and why I no longer considered myself Roman Catholic. You were afraid for my immortal soul, so I told you that that was none of your business. That was between me and my God, I told you, and to my surprise, you backed off.

Following the feast on Easter Sunday, it was customary for the family to go to the beach on Easter

Monday, a public holiday. What happened that day cemented the craziness of living under your roof; the hypocrisy, the double standards, the pettiness of the mob.

You'll remember that the day turned out to be cool and overcast, but that didn't matter, we were going to the beach anyway, as we always did.

It was merciful, because to stay at home another day in the hothouse that was our family home was unbearable.

The ring-around in the extended family started early.

A group finally came together, and we all drove in convoy to the familiar beach on the Sunshine Coast.

Eventually, there would be your brother Cesare and his family of five, your sister Giuseppina and her family, your parents, and seven of us, including George. All in all, more than twenty people came together for a day at the beach.

We never went out alone as a family. Dad always

had to have a posse of people with him, to hold his hand, in case something happened and he didn't know what to do.

Being alone at home was one thing; being out alone as a family was another, as there was no let-up from the tension of home. At least with others around, I saw you both laugh and the pressure of home diminished, even if it was just for a few hours.

At twenty-two, I was the eldest of the second generation in the extended family. The cousins were much younger, more boisterous, and poor company for young adults. But of course, I had to go along, I couldn't stay home with George. We'd have been alone all day!

Imagine what could have taken place! Imagine the gossip!

On arrival, the men set up camp while the women busied themselves with putting coffee and morning tea on the table. Once cleared away, the men took out a pack of cards and began playing *Scopa*.

Then the women got together to gossip about

the children, old times, and whoever or whatever was topical that day. The children went down to the water's edge and played in the sand.

George and I didn't fit in with any of those groups and we were left alone. No one invited George to play cards. No one even spoke to him. It was clear that we were going to have to entertain ourselves.

I looked around at the scene in front of me, remembering the numerous times I had been at that beach when I had wandered off by myself to sit on a rock, far away from the squawking flock of people, and look out over the vast expanse of blue water, slipping into a delicious state of daydreaming.

That day, though, the sea was choppy and grey, reflecting the sky above.

Only a few small groups of people were there that Easter Monday, dotted along the esplanade. Although the threatening rain kept many people away, I was grateful to be there just the same.

Everyone wore warm cardigans and jackets as

a buffer against the wind. I was wearing the very first pair of blue jeans I'd ever been allowed to buy, topped off with a sweater. George, more used to the cold than I was, wore a light long-sleeved shirt, jeans, and a light jacket. His appearance hadn't changed much in the six months since he'd been away. The one concession he'd made was to clip his beard so that it was now shoulder-length rather than halfway to his navel.

I don't think that made George look any less a hippie in Dad's eyes though, did it?

You and your sister were traipsing around after your elderly mother trying to make her comfortable. Your father, as the elder statesman in the family, talked down to the men as they took turns to play their hand. The games got quite loud and heated at times, all in Sicilian.

FIFO seemed to be the motto of the day: Fit In or Fuck Off.

So we did.

We went for a walk on the beach.

Out of their line of sight, we began walking on the sand, carefully picking our way through shards of glass, pieces of faded coral, and jellyfish that had been swept up onto the beach.

We began talking about the scene we had just left behind.

Oh, how I hated that scene. They were raucously loud, and there were too many prying eyes. Even though they were watching their cards and their children, I knew they were watching me and George.

After a while, I realised we were further than I'd ever been before on my own, so we decided to turn back.

"Don't want to set tongues wagging," I said to George.

Each moment we had alone together was precious, and neither of us really wanted to go back.

When I eventually arrived back at the camp-site, I noticed immediately that something had changed.

The men were still playing cards, but you were sitting in the back seat of the car, wearing that face I knew only too well: the glare, that worrisome expression, the face of martyrdom.

Suddenly, the familiar guest was with me again... that sickening feeling of anxiety, dread and foreboding in the pit of my stomach. I turned to look into the faces of the other women, my grandmother, my aunts, and I knew something was up.

Your sister-in-law was trying to cheer you up, her edgy laughter betraying her nervousness. She gave me a look that conveyed unspoken accusations.

All those years of observing my captor were about to pay off.

"*Chi c'è,*" what's up? I asked innocently.

"Where have you been?" you demanded. "The children, your cousins, went out looking for you, and they came back after an hour saying they couldn't find you."

You have always been prone to exaggeration when it suited you.

I knew that ten-year-old girls didn't walk half an

hour each way looking for us. At most they would have been gone twenty minutes in total.

I knew you were playing at something.

"Did they find it?" I asked hastily.

Bewildered, you asked, "Find what? What are you talking about?"

"My watch, the gold watch you gave me on my twenty-first birthday! George and I have spent the last half hour looking for it in the sand. Did they find it?" I blurted.

"That Italian gold watch? Why are you wearing it here anyway? How did you lose it?" you demanded, hooked into my little ruse.

I looked into the faces of your support group and could see from their eyes that the children had not reported finding any watch.

"Lunch is ready, and we've been waiting for you. You can take the kids with you after lunch to look for it again." The expression on your face changed from one of betrayal to concern for the 'lost' piece of jewellery.

Crisis averted, I thought.

You left the car and put lunch out on tables spread with tablecloths and set with napkins, cutlery, and glasses.

George bent over to whisper in my ear, "What was that about losing a gold watch?" George had studied Latin at school.

"That was a red herring," I whispered back.

"A red herring? What does a herring have to do with a gold watch?" he asked, clearly perplexed by this turn of phrase.

"I said I'd lost my watch to divert her attention. She was lying about the kids looking for us for over an hour. She and all the others thought that you and I were having sex in the sand dunes."

"Really? What a missed opportunity!" George confided, his smile camouflaged by his ample moustache.

I knew that in front of your parents, you were concerned about the possible loss of my chastity, and about your family's honour.

"Where is the watch?" George continued.

"In my pocket," I replied. "I didn't want to justify myself to her in front of all these people. It's none of their business. I'll go onto the beach again after lunch and miraculously find it."

I had got away with it — for now. But deep down, I knew that the crisis had only been kicked further down the road. It had not been averted.

The dread in the pit of my stomach got worse as the day progressed. Not knowing how things would turn out at home made me feel sick all afternoon.

Yet a part of me saw the funny side of it as well, the thought they'd had that we were in the dunes making love almost under their noses.

They're jealous, I thought. They hadn't been able to do anything like that during their engagements, and they didn't want to allow me that freedom, even as an adult.

Thinking about the women there that afternoon

put a fleeting *Mona Lisa* smile on my face. Like the old women sitting outside their homes in ancient Sicilian villages, they observed everything and everyone around them. Any whiff of scandal would have given them an opportunity to gossip,.

Here I was, a university graduate, the first female in the family with such a distinction, over the age of 21, going alone for a long walk with her fiancé unchaperoned. Maybe he had stolen a kiss? Maybe we had gone all the way?

I could see their minds working overtime, their hearts all aflutter, all in a tizz...

As they thought, so must it be true.

A whirlpool of acid had now replaced lunch in my stomach, whipped up with each accusatory glare from the women.

No one spoke during the drive home.

When we arrived home, George was invited in. You and I prepared dinner. I was on edge, the hairs standing up on the back of my neck. I had no idea how this was going to turn out. Even seeing the funny side of it did not protect me from what was going to happen.

Dad and George sat together at the kitchen table, where all-important conversations took place in the family—Dad at the head of the table and George beside him.

"Let me explain something to you, George," Dad started. "In Sicilian families, we don't do what you did today. When a young couple is going to be married, there must always be a chaperone present. I am telling you this because you are not one of us, because you are a foreigner and I don't expect you to know. But Francesca should know this, and she should not have done what she did today."

It's my fault... again. My heart rate picked up pace.

God, I can't wait to get out of this house, I thought.

What is so goddamn wrong with going for a walk with your fiancé after you haven't seen him for six months?

"When you get married, you can do whatever you want to do, go out whenever you want. But until then, you do things our way. This is our way; we've done it this way for hundreds of years. I know things are different where you come from, but this is Sicily here in this house. Can you agree to this?"

George agreed. Dad told you to get a bottle of wine. Pouring a glass for himself and one for George, the men drank in silence.

I could breathe again.

Dad had acted in a way I hadn't expected. At least there were no terrible consequences.

The next morning, you told me, you received phone calls from your mother and your sister Orazia, who, on hearing what Dad had done, labelled him a coward. They told you that Dad should have sent George packing for what he had done, that it was unforgiveable, that my honour was now in question... and on it went.

But I remember you were also relieved at Dad's measured reaction.

And your family?

You told them to go take a cold shower.

I was very proud of you then.

But your mistrust of me remained.

Even if I had done everything according to your wishes and demands, would you have trusted me more?

I don't think so.

The next time George and I met in secret, we talked about what had happened.

He told me that he understood, but that he was only going along with the games because he wanted me. He wasn't marrying you or Dad, or *la famiglia*.

He had come back for me only.

And if that was what he had to do in order to get me, that's what he would do.

This Protestant Lutheran had agreed to something he'd thought he would never agree to in his whole life: marry into the Roman Catholic Church.

George then told me what had happened during the six months he was back in his home country.

When he returned to his family, word got around that he had met someone he was going to marry. And horror of horrors, she was Roman Catholic!

"One weekend," George told me, "my mother and I were summoned to our clan's ancestral home to meet with my extended family and discuss this 'travesty'. Over two hundred people turned up. We Protestants had fought against Roman Catholics and the Roman Catholic pope for hundreds of years, and we're proud of our Protestant heritage. So a Protestant marrying a Catholic is heresy in my family.

"But I'd told my immediate family about you beforehand," George continued, "and they supported me. I discovered at the family meeting that I had to get family dispensation to marry a Catholic. I couldn't believe that this was still happening today, but it was. Our family is fiercely protective of our Protestant heritage."

It seemed that the Protestant–Catholic war was on again. Perhaps it had never ended.

I looked at George, this long-haired, bearded, hippie traveller who appeared to have shed the shackles binding him to society, and saw that he was still facing some long-standing beliefs in his family as well.

It didn't end there.

As a Roman Catholic, I was also required to get special dispensation from the Catholic Church to marry a Protestant!

And I wasn't even a regular churchgoer!

This stand-off had been going on for five hundred years.

"It wasn't easy persuading them of my intentions and getting the family's approval," George continued.

"Why is it such a big deal in your family?" I asked.

"My ancestors were among the original families to convert to Lutheranism," he told me. "Because of the religious intolerance of the Catholics around them, the Lutheran pioneers had to leave their homes and move to another place where their new faith was tolerated. My family has long suffered from religious intolerance from Catholics and the Catholic clergy, so when one of us wants to marry outside the faith, it's a big deal."

And I thought my family was stuck in the past!

After that day at the beach, Dad acted cool, calm, and disinterested, as per normal. He never sat with George and talked to him again or took the time to get to know him. Wedding preparations were underway, but he said nothing, did nothing. He just let us get on with things.

We were making plans to spend his money on my wedding, and he provided no guidelines or suggestions and gave no input.

It seemed to me that he saw his role as just turning up, walking me down the aisle, and paying the bill.

I often wondered at the time and years later why Dad showed no interest in George at all. Not to try to get to know the man who would marry his daughter seemed at odds with what I thought his job was as a father. Why did he always just ignore George?

At first, I thought that he was always dog-tired after a day's work. But his approach to George was consistent and persistent. So I began looking a little deeper.

Perhaps it was that an Austrian was the last

person he had expected to invade his inner sanctum? Perhaps he had washed his hands of all responsibility for this marriage, which allowed him to lay blame on the 'guilty' parties if something went wrong.

At first, I was relieved at his lack of interest, that I didn't have to deal with him. Then I became concerned, because I didn't know what he would be comfortable with in terms of the wedding. After weeks of his showing no interest in this marriage or wedding preparations, I started to become jittery.

Why did he show no interest? I felt like he was giving me enough rope to hang myself, and then, when he was good and ready, he would tighten the noose. Was this the hunter watching the hunted again? Did he expect me to know what he had in mind without ever telling me?

The old sense of dread returned. I was again the ever-vigilant 'hunted', under the Sword of Damocles, and I had no idea what the trigger might be or when it would happen. I just knew that he would get me on something, even though I was very careful to keep to the rules, as I understood them.

And he did.

One day I told you that George and I were going shopping for engagement rings. You told me you wanted to come along, but I replied that we wanted to do this on our own. You weren't happy about the arrangement, but as we were adults, I didn't see anything wrong.

We went out together, bought the rings, and showed them to you and Dad that night.

Neither of you said anything, but the look on your face and Dad's told me something was wrong. In the buzz of the preparations for the engagement party that was held at home, I forgot all about it. Close family and relatives were invited.

For days beforehand, you were cooking, baking, and preparing. This was going to be a typical Sicilian family banquet.

During the meal came the time when it was customary for the groom to give a small speech and place the engagement ring on his fiancée's ring finger. Not knowing what to do or how to do it so that it would be acceptable to you and him, or whether Dad would get up and say a few words, George just got up, said a few words, and put the ring on my finger. I then did the same.

Then Dad picked himself up and spoke his mind for the first time after months of silence.

He voiced his disappointment and his anger that I had gone out to buy the engagement rings without at least one of my parents being present to supervise, approve, and purchase the groom's engagement and wedding rings.

That was the first time I'd heard of this custom! So much for his announcement that I was an adult and could make my own decisions!

He didn't expect that George would know what was customary in the family, as an outsider. But he did expect me to know.

How could I have known, when I was the first to get engaged with family approval? How could I have known when neither he nor you had told me about the custom?

I had knowingly and shamelessly gone out and broken the custom, he went on.

This engagement therefore did not have his blessing.

I had just one wish—for the ground to open up and swallow me alive.

No one knew what to say or where to look. Not even you.

Finally, *Nonna* Mariuzza spoke up. She told him to calm down, that it was all done now. "They're adults," she said. "You can't expect everything to be done the way it used to be done thirty years ago," she said.

But he'd had his vengeance.

Next day, everything was back to normal. He said nothing, ignored me and George, and fell asleep in front of the television.

Status: normal.

In hindsight, perhaps it was because your mother,

the powerful matriarch of the family, had poured soothing oil over the troubled waters that there were no further major upsets in this strange courtship.

How was I to know how to behave in this strange world where nothing was communicated?

I was again navigating my way through a mine-field with an outdated map.

The next argument was over the dress. There was no question of buying it off the shelf — it was to be a one-off. We went to Edwards' Emporium where I selected the design, and then you and I selected the fabric and all the accoutrements.

When it came to choosing the fabric, I decided on a shade of ivory.

You went ballistic.

"No daughter of mine is getting married in... what do you call it... ivory?" you hissed under your breath. "That's a dirty colour, that's not pure white."

"What's the big deal, Mum?" I asked innocently.

"Don't you know? *La sposa*, the bride, always wears white. It's a reflection of her purity. We can't let people think anything else."

"So it's for *l'occhio sociale*?

"Certo, of course," you said matter-of-factly.

"It doesn't matter what I want, does it?" I replied with a hint of frustration.

You turned to face me: "We can't let people think anything else."

I continued, "They're going to think what they want anyway."

"We are not going to give your father, or anyone else, any reason to think otherwise," you declared with finality.

With that implied threat, the matter was settled.

And with that, I made another concession to the law.

I came to realise only much later in life how macchiavellian things really were in our family. The law was almighty, all-pervading, all-seeing, ever-present, always monopolising people's thoughts, feelings, behaviour. I could have been talking about God, for that's what the law felt like. However, I never knew of its existence until I wanted to do things differently. Of course, I was always wrong, and made to feel wrong. Even for wanting to design and create my wedding according to *my* dreams.

Your view was that as your daughter, it was my job to honour my parents for giving me life and for raising me. I was expected to show gratitude. The way to honour you was to display my gratitude and fulfil all the customs and rituals of marriage as had been done for generations before.

I had no say. It didn't matter what I wanted.

Clearly in our family it didn't matter that democracy had won over dictatorship in 1945. You still lived your lives, and still raised your families, based on feudalism. Democracy was for everybody else.

In this family, it was as if I was tied to the end of a piece of rope. I was let out into the world of democracy with enough 'rope' and told that I could make my own decisions and go my own way as an adult. Then some all-powerful force would yank the rope whenever it chose, when I least expected it, and haul me back behind the fortress of feudalism and patriarchy.

The conflict between feudalism and democracy was still going on in the 1970s.

Now, after years of reflecting on the past and our connected lives, I understand that you and your *paesane*, your countrymen, could no more suddenly become democratic after the war than I could become a feudal serf, despite all the family's attempts to make it happen.

You wanted me and all your children to honour you, the same as in a feudalistic society, simply because you fed and clothed us and provided us with an education. You would be seen as successful 'honourable' people. And I'm sure that within your family and social circles, you were.

In a modern democracy, that is the least that is expected of parents.

I was also conditioned to play my part and ensure the continuation of feudalism, where men reigned supreme and women were their possessions to do with as they wished. You put a noose around my neck, tied my hands behind my back, tied my ankles together, and placed me on an unstable, wobbly chair. Then you told me that if I lost my balance and hung myself, Dad would kill you because it would emasculate him in the eyes of the Sicilian community. It was my job to keep my balance on that chair, so I wouldn't fall. There is nothing worse than a fallen woman, in the eyes of Sicilians. A fallen woman is expelled from the family and society, unaided and unsupported. A fallen woman is allowed to hang, while everyone turns their backs and lets her die.

In order to live, and for you to live, I had to stand still, hands and feet bound, on an unstable footing.

A woman who survived this treatment was considered honourable and therefore fit to be a wife and mother.

But it doesn't end at marriage, even though mothers tell their daughters that they can do as they wish after marriage. Women must continue standing on that chair after marriage. They cannot fall.

And so the practice of entrapment passes from mother to daughter through generation after generation.

When I asked you why things were as they were, I received no answers that could satisfy me. You just looked away with helplessness written all over your face.

"*Per l'occhio sociale*, for society. This is how it must be, if you want to get married with the peace and blessing of the family."

Do you realise that you owe me your life?

I saved you as a child when I stood in front of you and shielded you from a bullet all those years ago. I've saved you ever since, by staying balanced on a wobbly chair with my hands tied behind my back and a noose around my neck.

Still, all that matters is that your family and the

Sicilian community see that I remained loyal to the family tradition. I just wanted to get married in peace... the alternative was unthinkable.

The next few weeks went by in a blur. The guest list had to be finalised and wedding invitations sent out. I wanted a small wedding with close friends and family; you and Dad wanted to invite extended family and friends, because you didn't want to offend anyone. A discussion had to be had with Dad, but he didn't have it with me. All communication with him passed through you, the relay station. Not surprisingly, you and Dad won. The guest list exceeded 200.

The bridesmaids' dresses... the flowers... the cake... the reception... the church... the church...

A marriage between a Roman Catholic and a Lutheran Protestant in the Roman Catholic Church was not going to be as easy as I thought.

We were required to attend pre-marriage

'counselling' sessions with the Catholic priest who would perform the marriage ceremony.

The sessions were held weekly for the six weeks before the wedding. They were intended to raise and discuss our beliefs, values, and expectations of each other, all those things that can turn a very happy wedding into a very sour marriage. One of the issues covered was the faith that any children we had would be raised in.

George was adamant that no children of his would be raised Catholic, and he received no argument from me. I was happy for our children to be raised Lutheran. But we couldn't share this with the priest, who wanted us to make a commitment that our children would be raised Catholic. George engaged the priest in a discussion about Catholicism and Luther, and by the end of the session, the priest had completely forgotten about the commitment. It never came up again, and we didn't sign away our rights to raise our children in whatever faith we saw fit.

It was after about the third session that Dad began to wonder what we were up to always on a Thursday evening, why I was coming home late from work, and always with George in tow.

He was not pleased. I know you had told him we were seeing the priest as part of pre-marriage counselling, but judging from Dad's reaction, he didn't believe you or me. That night, he threw a tantrum and spoiled the evening for everybody, again.

Had we, hadn't we?

That was the question that plagued his over-active imagination.

Then finally the week of the wedding arrived. Dad still hadn't spoken to us.

Every night during the week before the wedding, guests brought their wedding gift to the bride's home, as was customary at that time.

Dad loved it. He was a gracious host, welcoming people, offering drinks, telling you to put on another pot of coffee, chatting, laughing. All the serious stuff had already taken place, all the planning had been done, and he just had to give me away and pay the bill. He was in his element.

As people arrived, you busied yourself ensuring the guests were well looked after, making many pots of espresso and putting out Sicilian *paste di mandorla* and *cannoli*.

You had set up a table in the dining room to hold all the gifts. It was my job, as the bride-to-be, to open the presents and put them on display with the card so I knew later who to send thankyou cards to.

This is the last leg, I thought. *I can get through this.*

It was custom at that time for newly married couples to be gifted furniture or homewares to furnish their new home.

But because we were going to live in Salzburg shortly after we married, we received gifts of homewares that could be easily placed in storage.

They were beautiful gifts. It seemed that the family was repaying some kind of debt to you, for housing and feeding them, and cleaning up after them in your home during the early years of your married life.

This system of obligation and duty, of repaying obligations, was something that made me uncomfortable. It felt like setting up for another round of obligations when their children married, and so on, ad infinitum.

As the table began to groan under the weight of the gifts, and the visitors came to inspect the gifts from other wedding guests, I observed a curious thing.

The womenfolk, the purveyors of the culture, the beliefs, values and expectations, stood in front of the tables surveying the gifts one by one.

What are they thinking, I wondered.

'How does my gift stack up against others?'

'Did I spend enough?'

'Am I going to be left behind?'

'Does my gift put my family's honour to shame?'

'Is my family going to be humiliated for not spending enough? Or have I spent too much?'

And then a tiny smile of self-satisfaction would creep over their faces when they realised that they had spent at least as much as this family member or that, a bigger smile if they realised they had spent more than others. That meant they were wealthier than others.

The family was playing a game of ostentation, who's got more money, who's made more progress since they've been in Australia. They measured their progress in terms of money and accumulated wealth that they could show off to others with pride.

Well, I thought, *they can play their games. I'll gratefully accept the gifts.*

I knew that I wouldn't be taking them with me overseas. They would all stay in storage until later. Many of them weren't taken out of their packaging until many years later.

It took me many years to realise that Sicilians weren't alone in playing such games. Australians did as well. I just didn't know it at the time. I looked to the Australian culture to model my life and values on.

I didn't realise at the time that many Australians also held ancient beliefs, especially towards women. Sicilians weren't alone in that.

It would take me many years to realise that domestic violence crossed cultural boundaries.

A couple of weeks before the wedding, George and I went out house-hunting. After the debacle over the engagement rings, we invited you to come along, and you did. Finally we found a lovely old Queenslander on a large block of land in the inner-city western suburb of Rosalie and rented it immediately. George moved in straight away. Typical of that time, rental houses were furnished: the kitchen was fitted out with a fridge, the small bedroom had a single bed and wardrobe, and the main bedroom had a double bed, a silky oak wardrobe and dresser. Just the basics. We only needed the essentials while we worked and saved up for our departure the following year.

Then I made another discovery, another custom that was a relic of a by-gone era.

Once we'd decided on the house, you checked it out more carefully, announcing that it would do just fine.

I looked quizzically at you and asked what you meant.

It was then you disclosed the next custom which I was expected to uphold.

"It is custom for the women closest to the bride to prepare the marital bed for the wedding night," you declared.

Continuing, you told me that it involved the bride's mother and mother-in-law coming together the day before the wedding and making the bed. The idea was to show the bride's dowry to her mother-in-law. The best linen from my glory box was to be used to make the bed, preferably linen that the bride herself had embroidered, as was the custom, and topped off with delicately embroidered covers. As my mother-in-law was in Austria and was not attending the wedding, you invited your mother, sisters, and sisters-in-law to attend this 'ceremony'.

Fly Francesca Fly

All I could do was shake my head in disbelief.

It seemed to me that the purpose of this bed-making ritual was to show the other members of the family how you were sending your daughter off.

I wasn't there—I wasn't allowed to be there—because only married women were allowed. I can only imagine the talk around the bed, the girly giggles, the double entendres.

Did they tell stories of their own wedding nights? Or was that sacrosanct, the holy of holies?

I hated the thought of all these women touching my bed, even being in that bedroom.

Did they give little yelps of joy to see beautiful fresh new linen?

Did you have morning tea at the house then too?

Clearly, neither George nor I had a say in the matter. The custom had to be obeyed.

My choices were: resist or accept.

I let it go.

I wasn't prepared for what came next though.

In the old country, the bride's mother would enter the bridal chamber the morning after the wedding night. If the sheet was bloodstained, as expected if she was a virgin, she would pull it off the bed and wave it outside the window for everyone to see.

Another variation of this custom was that the sheet would be taken off the bed and shown to the bride's mother-in-law, proving that her daughter had indeed been a virgin at marriage.

All the agreements of property exchange and dowries hinged on that one thing: that the bride was a virgin at marriage, that she'd had no other lovers, that any children of this marriage were the groom's and his alone. This was all-important for matters of inheritance, but also honour. If a young bride was found *not* to have been chaste at marriage, there would be serious consequences.

The groom had the right to have the marriage annulled, and the father and brothers of the bride had the right to either kill her, or at the very least, ostracise her from the family. As a fallen woman, she would deserve that.

So much hinged on whether the crisp, new, meticulously embroidered, perfectly white, linen sheets were stained with fresh virginal blood.

No one questioned this centuries-old practice of proving the virginity of brides at the time of marriage, even though medical science had proven the practice to be based on myth.

You and Dad would come early the morning after the wedding to bring us coffee and breakfast, you continued.

That was the custom. As you blithely announced what you were going to do, I was roiling with rage.

"You will not be going into my bedroom, and you will certainly not be looking at, removing, or in any way doing anything with the sheets on my bed," I told you.

You were stunned.

"That's the custom."

"I don't give a shit about the custom," I replied. "It's all about you, and your medieval thinking about women.

Women's only value in your society is in their virginity, and nothing else. You attach so much importance to that — what about the man's virginity?"

"Well no, that's not important. Men are supposed to sow their wild oats before marriage."

"These practices are so oppressive to women," I said. "There are two sets of standards and they keep women suppressed, oppressed, and second-class citizen. Once she has given up her virginity, her life becomes one of drudgery, meaninglessness, and servitude."

I would see this very starkly in Sicily itself in later years.

I had been thinking about these things for a long time, all through my adolescence, in fact. I'd seen how you and other women lived, and while these women wanted for nothing, they were still in prison.

That was not going to happen to me.

Clearly it wasn't enough that I was the first female in the whole family to achieve a university degree, and with honours, even though in the minds of some

Sicilians I was a whore because it was their belief that females attending university were whores. My qualification was not enough honour for my parents.

"You will not be inspecting my bed the day after my wedding night," I repeated.

"Well, it's not so much for our benefit," you said calmly. "It's for your in-laws' benefit, but they're not here, and they don't hold to such customs anyway, coming from north of the Alps," you said.

"You bet they don't," I replied. "They're more enlightened. They live in the twentieth century! You live in another world, in another time. That's not where I live. I've grown up in this world here in Australia, and those practices don't have any meaning or importance here and now. I will not allow you to impose your ancient customs on me and my husband."

The more I attacked your customs, rituals, and beliefs, the more you clung to them. You slipped into the safety of that world, knowing that it didn't matter what I said, or how angry or disappointed I became, it would make no difference to the outcome. The law would have its way.

You agreed, somewhat reluctantly.

Early on the morning after the wedding, you and Dad came bearing coffee-making equipment to make the strong, aromatic, black espresso and breakfast. We had breakfast together on the veranda, you and Dad, George and me.

As we made small talk with our coffees, there came a knock at the door.

Who could that be? I wondered.

I looked quizzically at you, Mum, but you looked away.

"Who is that?" I asked you.

"It'll be your *Nonna* and your Zia Orazia," you replied sheepishly.

After our conversation about this, you still went ahead and agreed to this? I thought. I could feel the lava deep inside me begin to well up ready to erupt.

I explained to George what was happening.

I was fuming, but when I looked at George to

see his reaction, I saw that he was calm and serene... and... was that a hint of a smile I saw at the corner of his mouth?

Before even coming to greet us, you led the women directly into the bedroom. You all came out happily chatting a couple of minutes later. You looked relieved.

Immediately on hearing the women's cheerful banter, Dad began to be friendlier, chatting with George, pouring coffee, inviting him to have another pastry.

After they all left, I asked George what had just happened, and why he was smiling like a Cheshire cat.

Once I had explained what a Cheshire cat was, he went on, "Well, like your Cheshire cat, I knew something they didn't. Of course I had something up my sleeve because I know of this custom. It's the same all around the Mediterranean. I just played the game. I wanted them to believe what they wanted to believe, so we could have our peace.

"I prepared some chicken blood before the wedding, and I sprinkled it on the bed because I knew they would come. Pity to soil those beautiful sheets though," he smirked.

We had the last laugh after all!

Chapter 23

Differences between my background and George's became much clearer to me on the occasion of my first Christmas in Salzburg.

Before I married, there was always mass to attend on Christmas Day, followed by a banquet at *Nonna* Maria's. While she lived, several families came together at her place; the other families were invited to lunch on New Year's Day.

After mass, we came home, changed, collected our gifts, and drove to your parents' place. Walking in through the front door was like walking into a Mediterranean marketplace. There was always the inevitable aromatic tomato sauce perfumed with basil and enriched with a Sicilian beef roulade called *farsumauro*. Growing up hearing the name of this dish over many years, I never thought twice about it. It was only as I got older that I discovered that the name referred to the Moors who had ruled Sicily more than a thousand years ago.

At *Nonna*'s, there was also the unmistakeable fragrance of homemade pasta or lasagne, and chickens roasting in the oven. In hindsight, as an adult, I admire her even more for cooking up the feasts she did in the small 1920's four-burner gas oven in her tiny kitchen on Australian Christmas days.

One particularly steamy Christmas Day, the mercury hit 40°C. On arrival at *Nonna*'s place, the men went to the ice-works to buy ice, and discovered that half of Brisbane had the same idea. By 11 o'clock the factory had shut its doors, leaving many hot, angry, and bewildered people to return to their celebrations empty-handed.

Christmas in the family always seemed like an

opportunity to gorge on food which, after the war, had become available all year round. Somehow, Christmas gave everyone permission to indulge. There was no mention of the birth of Christ in anything we did or said after attending mass.

Christmas usually spilled over into Boxing Day when everyone would meet at *Nonna*'s place at 7 in the morning, drive to the beach in convoy, and continue the indulgence there. As a youngster, it was all very exciting. As I entered my teens, it was all a bit embarrassing.

George's family lived in the American occupation zone at the end of the war. Austria had been divided into sectors by the four victors: America, France, Britain, and Russia. This four-power occupation of Austria ended in 1955, so children growing up after the war in the American sector were educated in the ways of democracy, American style. Their history books were vetted and approved by the American occupation forces, and they were immersed in the ideas of personal freedom and responsibility. After hundreds of years, Austrians were finally coming out from under the yoke of empire, aristocracy, and dictatorship that had brought their country to its knees.

Ordinary people, freedom-loving people, could now create and pursue their lives under the protection of a democratic constitution, experiencing political freedom and freedom of speech for the first time ever. They witnessed religious freedom again; they experienced the freedom to pursue their interests, their creativity, and their happiness. The country flourished.

Christmas had always held great religious significance in this country. In George's family, Christmas was about living the meaning of the season and sharing the day with family and loved ones. Compared to Christmas celebrations in our family, their celebrations were very low-key.

I cherished Christmas in George's family while we lived there. I came to love the weeks leading up to Christmas—the snowfalls transforming the city and countryside into a magical wonderland; rugging up against the cold; the fragrance of coffee, cinnamon, and cloves mixing and wafting in the air from the *Kafés* and *Konditoreien*; fairy lights, twirled around trees and light posts, twinkling warm white from dusk each afternoon; church bells tolling every hour on the hour; the Salzburg Christkindlmarkt in *Domplatz* (Cathedral Square) with its colourful market stands selling traditional Christmas tree decorations, regional handcrafts, and of course, delectable Austrian specialties and mulled wine; the *Krampus* parades; and traditional music and choral singing.

Even the laid-back Christmas Eve when the family sat around the candlelit Christmas tree, decorated with hand-made decorations and baubles, with a family member playing *Stille Nacht, Silent Night*, on the piano, and small gifts shared around, was a novel experience for me. A light supper was followed by attending midnight Lutheran Church service together.

This felt how family life should.

Much of the difference between George's family

and ours was due to our different cultures: his Teutonic background versus our Mediterranean background.

Visiting Sicily in the late 1970s was an eye-opener for me. We hired a little Fiat 500 to drive around the island. As we rounded a bend on a narrow, unsealed mountain track, we nearly collided with another road user — a mule-driven cart. The old man leading it wore a torn old hat over his heavily lined and stubbled face. In the back of the cart sat a woman wearing black robes from head to foot with only a mesh covering her eyes. I know now that this robe was a burqa. I was astonished to see a woman dressed like this in late-twentieth-century Sicily. In some small mountain village, ancient Moorish practices lived on, it seemed.

Even day-to-day experiences showed me how different Sicilians were from me and from northern Europeans. A conversation with a local seven-year old girl in Sicily left me speechless. Out of the mouth of that child I heard the fatalism that Sicilian mothers pass on to their daughters, preventing any sort of change from taking place. There was no doubt in my mind that the young girl would grow up to be just like her mother.

The legacy of Austria's history was written in its people as well.

When George was growing up, his next-door neighbours were the Horvath family. The father was a regional medical officer, while his wife was a stay-at-home mum, like most women at that time. Their son, Sebastyan, was the same age as George, and they were best friends. Seb's father came from a long line of nobility under the Austro-Hungarian Empire. Even though the monarchy fell in 1920, Seb's father still thought of himself as an aristocrat, and expected to be treated accordingly.

Titled Austrians insisted on being called by their full appellation, like 'Herr Doktor Horvath', Mr Dr Horvath. Those without such a distinction were expected to bow deferentially when addressing nobility, as had been custom for centuries.

As George and Seb were growing up, Seb confided to George that his father used to beat him regularly with a whip or a leather belt. Seb was never good enough for his father; he never received grades that were high enough, even if he achieved ninety-nine per cent in a subject.

When he was sent to boarding school in Switzerland to finish high school, Seb rubbed shoulders with the sons and daughters of Europe's now-defunct aristocracy. He loved that he had access to such circles and took pride in introducing George to his new friends.

When Seb began studying medicine at university, his father mocked his son's attempts to excel. One day, after Seb had been whipped quite severely, George had had enough. He demanded of Seb's father that he stop beating his friend. The old man reached for his whip to lash George, but George dashed forward, grabbed the old man's arms, preventing him from using the whip. Looking him straight in the eye from that position, George told him that this was a taste of what he would do if he ever heard again that Seb had been whipped.

When I heard the story, I wondered why Seb couldn't or wouldn't defend himself against his own father, why he allowed his father to whip him still, even in his twenties.

Fast-forward thirty years. Seb was a qualified medical practitioner and scientist with not one but two doctorates. He had to achieve higher than his father to prove that he was at least as good as his father. Seb had a thriving research business and was highly sought-after for his specialised skills, not just in Austria but throughout the world.

The next time we met up with Seb, he was married with twin boys aged five. We met only one of the boys though. The other had been sent away to live with Seb's uncle, his father's youngest brother. Seb and his wife kept the 'good' child for themselves, handing the 'bad' boy over to his uncle to raise. Seb believed that his 'bad' son needed some of the child-rearing 'guidance' that his own father had used on him, which he knew his uncle still practised.

Despite the long-standing friendship, George decided he could no longer be friends with Seb.

George had taken several years out of his career to find himself in the world. Seb used that same time to pursue his doctorates. In his fifties, Sebastyan Horvath was still trying to please Daddy.

Chapter 24

I never wanted to come back to Australia, Mum.

Did you know that?

I cried floods in the weeks leading up to our departure. I wept rivers in the weeks after we returned, for leaving Europe, for leaving George's family who so wanted us to stay.

For the first time in my life, I had felt enveloped in a big warm protective bear-hug in that place, in that family. And I was doing the unthinkable – leaving.

Why didn't I want to come back?

Simple. I knew what I was coming back to.

I knew that nothing had changed between us. I knew that the family hadn't changed in that short time. I knew I would have to deal with, and probably argue with you, over your Sicilian child-rearing practices with my children.

I knew that life was never going to be easy with you and Dad. Our children were your first grandchildren, the first ones to try your Sicilian ways on. That we would be living in the same city meant there would be enough opportunities for differences to arise between us.

Why did I come back then?

I knew I had to face the very things I had been trying for years to avoid: my fears.

As an adult, I had to deal with them. While I had physically left the golden cage, in my head and my heart I was still inside that cage. If I was ever going to be truly free, I needed to return and work through all that still held me captive.

When we left Australia, I was a newly married girl. On our return, I was the mother of two children. I expected that George and I would be respected as the heads of our family, that we would determine what went on in the life of our family, as we had experienced in Salzburg with friends and family alike. I expected that you and Dad would respect the independence and sovereignty of our own separate family, and that we would make our own decisions about what was right for our family... as you had told me before I was married.

It didn't take me long to realise I was expecting too much.

The differences between you and Dad and George and me were not just cultural or religious. They were also personality differences, which I began to experience shortly after we returned.

After we bought our first home, a 1920's Queens-lander, life began to settle down somewhat — raising children, paying the mortgage, learning to relate to you and Dad again. You were the most doting grandparents, too much sometimes. There were changes that all of us had to learn to negotiate. But of course, I had forgotten — there was no negotiation with Dad. Just compromise, from me, if I wanted peace between us.

When he saw danger or risk to the children, he

couldn't help but speak up, not in their defence but in criticism of us as parents. As the children got older, we bought them bikes which they loved riding around the yard and later, for exploring the local area. They always had bicycles, even into their teens. Dad thought bikes were too great a risk. But George and I took the view that with training and supervision, bicycles were a way for children to learn mastery, self-control, discipline, and responsibility.

"Of course they could have an accident on the bike," George told Dad, "but they could have an accident just by walking across the street as well. We're not going to wrap them up in cotton wool because there's a slim chance they could have an accident."

Dad didn't like it. He didn't have to.

I compromised and bit my tongue many times in those years after our return. Like when you came to visit, and Dad would simply go to the bush lemon tree and break branches off that he thought needed pruning. At first I offered him a pair of secateurs to cut them off and was roundly criticised for thinking I knew more about pruning fruit trees than he.

The idea of asking permission to do something never crossed his mind.

Some things are just not worth fighting over, I used to think.

Once, when we had some of George's relatives from overseas staying with us, Dad turned up at our house with six live chickens. He thought that as we had a big family to feed, he would help by donating the chickens.

What a kerfuffle that was!

The chickens were squawking and flying around the back yard desperately trying to get away, while we all stood on the balcony overlooking the yard in disbelief. I wondered what George's relatives thought.

As he caught each chicken, he twisted its neck and hung each one upside down by the feet on the frame of the children's swing. When all six were hanging in a row, he looked up at his handiwork, satisfied, and announced, "There now, you can all have a feed." And left.

Everyone was stunned, but I was mortified. George and I exchanged knowing glances. We both knew Dad could be mercurial, but this time he had outdone himself. No one said anything for a few tense moments.

Then eight-year-old Albert broke the silence with his assessment of the situation. "Does this mean that we can now call Nonno 'Chook Dundee'?"

Even our overseas visitors had seen the movie *Crocodile Dundee*, and we all burst out laughing.

Out of the mouths of babes, I thought as I hugged him.

What could I say to our visitors, Mum?

'That's just my father. No, that's not how we usually get our chickens. We usually buy them at the supermarket.'

Still, there were dead chickens waiting to be dealt with, and the day was only getting warmer. By the time the debacle was over, the chickens were spoiled because they hadn't been bled immediately.

I'm sure he meant well. His generosity had got the better of him though. I'm sure that if he had shared his idea with you before acting on it, you would have had something to say about this harebrained idea!

George and I had again witnessed Dad conducting himself in our family life as if we were an extension of him.

All those years before I'd married, he had said over and over, "While you live under my roof, you live by my rules. When you are married, you can do whatever you like in your own home."

He never said though, that he could do whatever he liked in *my* home.

The biggest clash between George and Dad was still to come, and it caused a rift between our families for weeks.

Chapter 25

In his late fifties, Dad was working on his last-ever construction job: your dream house.

In the laundry, he wanted to use the concrete tubs that George and I had in our garden. We had planted them with herbs — parsley, basil, thyme, dill, and mint — and placed them at the bottom of the back steps close to the kitchen. These pre-war dual tubs were very sturdy, but they were not easily available any more. By this time, light stainless-steel laundry tubs were being installed in newly constructed homes. Except Dad. He liked concrete. He had worked with it since he was ten years old. And the tubs were free.

Dad had spoken with George about the tubs, and

George told him he could have them. He asked only that Dad let us know when he needed them so that we could empty them out and replant the herbs elsewhere in advance.

One morning, around 6.30, Dad arrived at our house. I was busy getting the children ready for school and feeding the baby, and George was getting ready for work. Ordinarily, Dad would pop upstairs into the kitchen, say hello to the kids, and tell us why he was there. That day, he did none of this. He made a beeline for the tubs and without warning, began ripping the herbs out of the soil and digging the soil out of the tubs. From the kitchen upstairs, I heard the noise and looked out to see what was going on.

I was horrified.

"What are you doing?" I called out.

"I'm taking the tubs. George knows; I talked to him about it," Dad replied, not stopping to talk.

I went inside and spoke with George.

"Do you know anything about this?" I asked.

"Well yes," George replied, "but I told him to let us know in advance, so we could empty the tubs ourselves and replant the herbs. What's going on?"

When I told George that Dad was pulling out the plants and taking the tubs, George turned bright red underneath his black beard and moustache. He pushed past me onto the landing at the top of the stairs. Down below, Dad continued his work.

"What are you doing, Paolo, coming here and just taking those tubs?"

"We talked about it, and you agreed," said Dad.

"I told you to let me know before you came so we could replant our herbs."

"Oh, that's just a bit of parsley and basil... you can grow them again anytime."

"That's not the point," continued George, getting more and more agitated. "This is not your property to do as you want. You could at least have come in and said 'Good morning' to your daughter and grandchildren. Now go! Leave my property!"

Dad collected his tools and placed them back in the wheelbarrow. As he turned to leave, I saw that his face had also turned bright red.

I felt the anxiety rise again in my throat. *What's going to happen now*, I worried.

He told you a version of this story that made sense to him. It seemed to me that Dad was a little intimidated by George with his wild-eyed look. George had intimidated men in many parts of the world with that look.

But when I heard what Dad told you, it was clear that he had missed the point altogether. He thought it was about the herbs. It was, in part. But more than that, it was about the fact that he was again doing as he pleased with our property. He didn't see anything wrong with what he had done.

Weeks passed. You sided with Dad; I stood with George, of course, even though I was immobilised by fear. I didn't know how to break the impasse with Dad.

One Sunday afternoon, we came to visit you. I let George do the talking, man to man. I felt like a typical

Sicilian woman in this situation, flitting around her children while the men talked serious stuff. It was clear that Dad would never see our point of view, so after each made his point again, George moved on, telling him he could come to collect the tubs.

"And next time, let us know in advance when you're coming, Paolo, so we can have it ready for you."

With that, the crisis was resolved. Dad ordered you to make pizza, pulled out a couple of beers for himself and George, and continued chatting as if nothing had happened.

He never did anything like that again.

For me, these two men in my life were like chalk and cheese: one I feared and despised, the other I loved but feared admitting, even to myself, the love I had for him. It was as if in admitting my love for George, Dad would disapprove. And I never knew what he would do if he disapproved of something I did. I do know though that I always felt I was walking on eggshells around Dad. He was very closed and secretive, rarely disclosing or discussing how he saw things, but roaring with rage when some invisible line or unspoken rule had been crossed.

Used to keeping his own counsel, he was by and large, unknowable.

Why didn't he approve my marrying George? He didn't say he disapproved, so it was left to me to read between the lines. I had to assume he accepted it, even if he didn't like it.

Maybe he was ashamed of my choice of husbands. He was not Sicilian, not Italian, nor even Australian. He was Austrian, for God's sake, a former WWII ally.

When we decided to marry, I assume that Dad thought he could either go along with this marriage, or withhold his approval and risk me eloping with George.

He must have thought that if he allowed the marriage and it didn't work out, he could always say that it had nothing to do with him. The failure of my marriage would not be his shame. But if I eloped with George, the shame for him would be great—and he still had another daughter to marry off.

He made his decision to allow my marriage based on what would be less shameful for him. It was a decision that carried with it minimal loss of face for him.

Do you think I'm being cynical now, Mum? Can you tell me when he ever showed any empathy, any consideration, at all, for anyone?

I didn't think so.

Now I understand why he had hoped George wouldn't return for me, and why he hoped I'd be unhappy in the marriage and leave.

But when we returned together with two young children, I guess he decided that the joy of having us back with grandchildren was greater than the feeling of shame he might still have been nursing. I suppose. I never knew. He never spoke to me about such things, or about anything.

When we returned, so did the hypervigilance, because I never knew what would set him off. Returning with a family was a new situation altogether and he hadn't changed in any of the ways that mattered.

When we announced to you and Dad that we were expecting our third child, I thought you might both express some joy for us, congratulate us, show some interest in this new grandchild.

What I saw from you, but mainly from Dad, made me feel twelve years old again.

The scowl on Dad's face made me feel that he didn't approve, and my heart sank. Suddenly a wave of heaviness, anxiety, and dread swept over me again. Why would I, a mature woman, feel like this again?

It was as if I had said, "I am pregnant, and I don't know who the father is," like I had broken some unspoken rule... again.

What fucking rule have I broken this time! The question screamed inside my head.

I decided that how you and Dad felt about this new grandchild was your problem, but it still gnawed away at me. By the time our fourth child was on the way, I didn't care how you and Dad felt about the pregnancy.

In the early years of our return from overseas, I often bit my tongue and said nothing directly to him, especially in the face of his disapproval. Speaking up hadn't worked in the past, and it wasn't working now either. I was just a female, except now I was my husband's chattel. And nothing I said mattered.

Only words spoken by men and actions taken by men mattered.

If Dad was ashamed of George, he couldn't really respect him. Could he?

Yet, living in Austria for many years I had grown accustomed to being listened to, to having a voice, to being respected and valued, to being accepted into George's circle of family, friends, and colleagues.

The differences between my experience north of the Alps and the Sicilian way became very clear from the first few days back in the 'bosom of my family'. In central Europe, people didn't just drop in to visit; they called before they came. They asked if they could hold my babies, and they respected the babies' need for rest.

Back here in Australia, the rellies started arriving whenever they wanted, in the typical Mediterranean fashion, without a thought to ring beforehand to see if it was convenient for us. Over time, this came to be quite an imposition, and we needed to have some control over our family life. We weren't just sitting around waiting for rellies to turn up to entertain them! So George made the first move and told them that they were welcome to come, just to call beforehand.

When they arrived, they would make a beeline for the bedroom to pick up the baby, just six weeks old at that time, whether he was awake or not. I did not matter. I was just the mother, after all.

It was a gradual re-education process that George and I embarked upon, and it wasn't easy. Even though I was married with children, educated, had lived overseas and thrived in a foreign country, I was still being treated as Sicilian women had always been treated.

I was not going to raise our children like Sicilians had been raising theirs for centuries. George and I chose to raise our children not according to tradition or the way things had always been done, but consciously, deliberately, and in their best interests.

That meant that we came into conflict with you and Dad many times over our children's upbringing.

It wasn't just the men who couldn't wrap their heads around the 'new' me. It was also the women. In fact, it seemed to me that the women were as stuck in the past as the men. Like you.

When I was in my 40s, you were still trying to tell me what to do. When I announced that I was returning to study, you scoffed at the idea, telling me to *fatti 'a quasetta* (go knit your socks), in anticipation of needing them in my old age which apparently, at forty, was fast approaching.

Was this how women kept other women in place in Sicily?

Instead of being the 'wind beneath my wings', from the beginning of my life you set out to be the withering Saharan *Scirocco*, the hot wind that blows periodically over Sicily from North Africa, scorching everything in its path.

Ironically, your opposition only strengthened my resolve to return to study. I didn't need your approval, although your moral support would have been nice, as I had supported you so often while I was growing up.

Chapter 26

Differences existed not only between George and Dad, and you and me, but also in your and Dad's approach to things, which caused conflict between you both.

Raised in an environment that rewarded shrewd resourcefulness, Dad had an expedient approach to his work. He never cut corners with foundations or with weight-bearing structures in the buildings he constructed. But outside that, he was always looking for ways to save money. His approach often resulted in having to dish out more money to fix a problem he had been trying to avoid in the first place. Where he could get away with doing things on the cheap, he did. This caused you no end of misery because you wanted things done properly the first time, and only once. You didn't necessarily want the most expensive tile-laying job on the floor of your new house; you just wanted it done properly. And if that meant paying a professional tiler to do the job, at a higher rate, then you were prepared to do so.

Dad selected the local handyman though, who ended up doing a disastrous job and costing you more in dollars and frustration than if he had retained a professional in the first place. Some of it could be salvaged, but most of the tiles had to be ripped up and the job redone.

Fortunately, it was his last project, but even that was not finished properly. He left entire areas of the house unpainted, internal fit-outs incomplete, landscaping unfinished.

Over the years, the money he saved on jobs was squandered on his trips back to Sicily where he showered family and friends with lavish gifts and an abundance of the best Sicilian specialties.

George was an honourable man, but very different from the Sicilian understanding of honour. In his work,

George espoused and practised excellence. No expedience or cutting corners. If something had to be done, it had to be done properly. People could die if he got something wrong. This attitude had been drummed into George, and all other children in his home country, from year one. Born into a culture of excellence, he challenged himself constantly to be better and do better.

This approach brought George on a collision course with Australian colleagues, workmates, and even clients. Australians had sayings like, "If it ain't broke, don't fix it," "She'll be right, mate," "Close enough is good enough," believing the advertising that told Australians, 'We are second to none'.

That saying got George's goat up big time. I was beginning to see the world through different eyes, Mum. I had joined my life with George's, and I suddenly needed to re-evaluate what I had always accepted and believed about this country and its people.

Over time I began to see that the 'she'll be right' approach at times came perilously close to 'shit'll be right', which sometimes put lives at risk.

Honour, for George, was about challenging himself to be the best he could be. It was not the type of honour that depended on imprisoning his wife to ensure that she didn't go astray so he wouldn't 'lose face'.

Where he also came into conflict with Australians was over his truth and honesty. His views didn't sit well with many people in his work life. His actions were consistent with his beliefs; he always did what he said he would do. He lived up to his standards and expectations of himself.

Along with the absence of self-deprecating humour, he found it a challenge to fit into Australian society.

I could handle his seriousness. What I needed, more than anything else, was a sense of safety, a feeling that the ground beneath me was not constantly shifting, and to be with someone as focused on setting high standards for himself as I was for myself.

I found myself falling in love with George more

and more every day.

The differences between George and the 'Sicilian way' spilled over into open conflict more than once. When I travelled for work, you interrogated George about why he allowed me to travel alone. All your fears spilled out: something might happen to *your* daughter; I might meet another man and have an affair...

Of course, George told you and Dad that he trusted me, and that I was safe.

That really blew your minds.

Yet, for us, trusting one another was the most natural thing in the world.

The darkest time in my adult life, in our relation-ship with you and Dad, came totally unexpectedly. We have never spoken about that time in any detail, Mum. I can tell you now though, that it was a very painful time in my life.

After we'd been married twenty years, George and I came face to face with your past and your Sicilian tradi-tions all over again. Old wounds reopened to disgorge the venom still deep inside, spilling over me and my family. It was a clash of belief systems: my beliefs based on personal accountability and self-determination, and your traditional Sicilian beliefs that your children were *always* your children and that they should continue to honour you by adhering to your code and your dictates, regardless of being adults themselves.

No one warned me about that!

After many years of hearing my cousin Angela's story of misadventure retold by bystanders and biased observers in the family, the opportunity arose to speak with Angela herself. I wanted to understand how much of it was truth, what were Chinese whispers, who had an agenda in this sad tale.

I already had four children by this time, and was in my forties.

I was aware of the antagonism between Angela's parents and you and Dad, but decided that this was your issue, not mine.

She had heard a lot about me too over the years.

We both had to get past our preconceived ideas about each other before we could speak freely with one another. I had hundreds of questions, and she wanted to download.

I came away with the view that she had shared the same outlook and problems I had as an adolescent growing up. And in some way, it was consoling to know that I wasn't alone in my struggles, Mum.

However, we chose different solutions to the unrelenting despair we felt as adolescents. Angela's choice of the traditional Sicilian *fuitina*, elopement, was a bolt for freedom at sixteen to get away from her parents and Sicilian law.

My path, including the education I pursued, resulted from my enduring belief that 'there must be another way'.

Of course, you came to hear about our meeting, and you were not amused. In fact, you were downright incensed that I had met with Angela. I was confused as to what I had done so wrong to cause so much bitterness. Hadn't you repeatedly told me when I was growing up that I could do what I wanted after I was married?

"You know what her father did to me and our family, don't you? You know we don't talk to that family. You know her father is a *vigliacco*. So why did you go meet with her? Why?"

"Yes," I replied, "I know what you have told me about that family and Angela's father. But I didn't meet him, or your sister. Angela is not her father or her mother. She and I are grown mature women now."

"If you want your father and me to come to your children's birthday party, you will promise me here and now that you will never see her again, that you will have nothing more to do with that woman," you threatened.

That hit me like a bolt of lightning and I suddenly saw very clearly.

Everything you and Dad had ever said about being able to do whatever I wanted once I was married was all a smokescreen. You never had any intention of letting me out of the cage that you had placed me in when I was growing up. It was always going to be like this. I was always going to be subject to arbitrary goalposts that shifted whenever, and wherever, you wanted.

And I would only ever have useless, outdated maps for a landscape that resembled the shifting sands of the Sahara.

I guess you expected that I would back down and agree to your terms just to have you attend the party. But I had already come a long way in creating a sense of stability in my life.

What you didn't realise is how excruciating the decades-long state of uncertainty had been for me. There was no way I would ever let you have power over me again.

"I'm sorry you feel that way, Mum. You and Dad are welcome to come to our children's party," I replied, "but I make my own decisions about who I see. That is not your choice. You no longer dictate to me who I can and cannot see."

With that, the die was cast.

But I didn't foresee what came next.

"Then you can forget that you have a mother and a father. You are not welcome in our house any more." You slammed the phone down. I was left holding the phone beeping the tone signalling disconnection.

When I told George what had happened, he congratulated me.

"Now you are free," he rejoiced.

"I suppose," I muttered.

So why did I feel like I'd swallowed hot lead again?

Even though I was in my forties, I was still obliged to defer to you as my moral compass. Clearly, I still had not done enough to honour you, or to earn my right to make my own decisions, even though I had always been told that I could do whatever I wanted after marriage.

My exile continued for more than three years, remember? Three years when we neither saw nor spoke with each other. You didn't acknowledge the birthdays of anyone in my family including the children. We didn't acknowledge yours. We remained distant for Easter, choosing to have family holidays by the beach instead. Christmas was the worst — we spent four Christmases alone.

Our children felt it strongly — they couldn't understand what had happened. They just knew that their grandparents had cut them out of their lives. The sense of abandonment I saw in their eyes was heartbreaking for me. They never really got over that time; they saw this incident as you using them as pawns to manipulate me.

George was a terrific support for me and the children, helping us all get through it.

But I felt it very deeply. In that moment when you passed judgement making me a *persona non grata*, I was eleven years old again, and my worst fears had come to pass.

I was an outcast, banished by my own parents.

I had dared to say no. I hadn't 'honoured' you and Dad by subjecting myself to your will and doing what you expected of me.

This family feud was one of those that could have easily continued through the generations. The story of *Romeo and Juliet* crossed my mind often in the aftermath of that phone call.

I stood my ground despite the grief it caused me and my family.

I didn't capitulate, even though it would have been easier to do so.

And George stood by me all the way.

I had fought so long and hard for the freedom to determine my own life and make my own decisions, I was not about to throw it all away just so that you would attend my children's party.

Their party was memorable — for your absence.

Then one day you called.

You told me that Dad was ill.

When we visited him in hospital as a family, the previous three years were washed away with tears.

But I had made my case.

Chapter 27

Years passed.

After our return from Austria, Dad saw that George was a family man, a principled man, a man not to be messed with, and his respect for George grew to the extent that he disclosed things about himself that he had told no one else. Dad was finally opening up.

For me though, the events of the early years of my life cast long shadows which never left me. There was a heaviness, a dense fog that engulfed me at all times. Occasionally I could push through it to the other side. For short bursts, the skies would clear, and the fog would transform into a high floating passing cloud, only to descend again another time. My children forced me to stay present to attend to their needs. Other times it was near impossible to jettison.

Eventually, my anxiety emerged in unexpected ways. When my youngest child was born, the bulimia started in earnest.

Growing up, I had developed an eating problem. You and Dad always encouraged me to finish the food on the plate. You'd never had enough to eat when you were growing up, you would say, and here I was leaving it on the plate.

So the guilts started there, reinforced by the teachings of the Catholic nuns at school.

The night I had stood in front of you to protect you cemented disordered eating. I would eat until I was so full I thought I'd explode. That feeling diverted my attention away from the god-awful feeling of being a target.

I realise now that that was the feeling addicts aspire to in order to escape the emptiness and despair that drives them to harm themselves with drugs, alcohol, food, gambling, overspending, anger, or self-mutilation.

I was harming myself by overeating, but how

could I have known? I was only twelve when it started.

My weight started ballooning, and you blamed me for eating too much.

I was caught in a vice: damned if I did, and damned if I didn't.

I didn't know how to stop overeating.

I gulped food down, especially when you and Dad argued, or when he got violent.

The problem eating was always at night, at dinner, when the family was together. My anxiety peaked between 6.00 and 6.30 every night, like a monster eating me up inside.

My body was my enemy, experiencing uninvited sensations that I had no control over and that I couldn't get rid of. My body attracted furtive, unwelcome glances from you and Dad, watching surreptitiously for signs of developing womanhood and of departure from the law.

My body was something to be ashamed of: I couldn't control its appetites, I couldn't control how it was changing.

I just wanted to be invisible, and the only way was by overeating.

Anxiety fuelled the overeating, and eating calmed the anxiety. As I got older, eating until I was more than full, I'd go to the bathroom, stick my fingers down the back of my throat, and vomit into the toilet bowl.

That's how I began to get some control over my weight.

I also began dieting in my teens, turning down your holy pasta and carbs, fighting you all the way.

In my teen years, I always saw myself as fat and ugly, and no boys would ever want me, or even look at me, because of that.

Your response, as usual, was glib.

"It's just baby fat. You'll grow out of it," you'd say, sweeping my concerns aside as if they were crumbs on the table.

During periods of high stress and anxiety, the eating disorder always returned, a constant companion, an unwelcome but familiar guest that exacted its price from me. Running away from it through overeating just fed the monster more.

Whenever I dieted and returned to my ideal body weight, I put the weight back on again, and then some.

I vowed over and over never to be the same size as you.

Chapter 28

In my fifties, I became ill for the third time in my life due to stress.

The lifelong anxiety, combined with PTSD, depression, and exhaustion finally caught up with me and I could no longer work.

Even after I began working on healing myself, there was still something else that I couldn't put words to.

For some time before I left my last job, I recognised that I was having memory problems. I couldn't remember whether I had done a particular task or not. Things would take me longer to do than most people. I needed extra time to get things together in my head, then I'd spend a lot of time double-checking.

Deep down, I knew I was in trouble. It had crept up on me over a long time, such that I couldn't remember when it had started.

I was terrified of finding out what was wrong.

I wondered if this was early onset Alzheimer's. So I did nothing. Classic head-in-the-sand response.

Then one day at work, my brain froze up: I couldn't think or do anything any more, like when a computer crashes and the screen freezes up.

I began dissociating, trying to get away, but I couldn't. I was having a panic attack, breathing in short, shallow breaths, reinforcing the panic.

I struggled to keep myself present in the job and I thought I was succeeding; others disagreed.

I couldn't remember things any more, things that had been discussed earlier in the day. I seemed to have no recollection of these discussions at all.

I was becoming less coherent in my conversations with people.

People around me looked at me quizzically,

wondering what was wrong with me.

The harder I tried to hide what was happening, the more stressed I felt, and the more obvious it became to others that I was struggling. But my job had to come first. "I'm ok, no, nothing's wrong," I said.

Yet at night, I would curl up in bed in a foetal position and cry myself to sleep, wishing not to wake up in the morning, wishing it all to be over.

Eventually I reached a point where I knew I had to change my life. My reactions were the same as those I'd had during and after the night that changed my life. I needed time to think, to understand what was happening to me, to recuperate and pick myself up again, so I could get back to work.

A couple of weeks off should do it, I thought optimistically.

I had to get to the bottom of the memory loss, the panic attacks, the dissociation.

A couple of weeks weren't enough though.

A couple of months, I thought. *Get some tests done,*

work out what's wrong, take remedial action.

How hard could that be?

I had tests done. Nothing explained the memory loss.

By then, I was distraught. Not knowing what was wrong. Not knowing how to tackle it. Not knowing how long I would need to recover.

A medical practitioner asked me where I wanted to be sent for further testing. That was the last straw. For Christ's sake, how the hell should I know?

Realising it was not going to be as easy as I had thought, I decided, reluctantly, to give up my job. I needed time out to look after myself and I had no idea how long it would take, or even if I would ever recover enough to be able to work again.

I drove to medical appointments all over town, but I shouldn't have. Driving through red lights because their meaning didn't register quickly enough, I had several near-collisions.

I had always been good at navigating using a

map, contrary to popular beliefs about women and map-reading, but in the headspace I was in, I couldn't navigate at all. I had to pull over to the side of the road, look at the map to work out where I was, and then figure out how to get home from there.

More than once, panic set in because I couldn't find my way to where I needed to be, even when I was on my way home. I would sit in the car, tears streaming down my face, not only because I couldn't find my way home, but because I recognised what it could mean, terrified that I might be experiencing signs of Alzheimer's.

I began looking for a medical practitioner who could give me some hope about getting to the bottom of my symptoms. Even after I found one and started having tests, it still took a long time to discover the cause of the problems, and even more time to find the appropriate solution.

One day I heard an interview with a young woman about her childhood experience of being sexually abused by Rolf Harris.

I was compelled to drop everything I was doing and listen to her. I began to feel increasingly uneasy. The feelings she described were what I was experiencing.

How could I be feeling the same way? I had no recollection of being sexually abused as a child. But I had experienced and witnessed things early in life that would today be classified as abuse.

And they predated 'that' night.

There was so much that I had wanted to forget, I had just buried it.

My recovery had to take place over time and on several levels—physical, emotional, psychological, and spiritual.

I could recuperate physically by taking the right meds. But recuperating psychologically, emotionally, and spiritually? That took a lot longer, and required that I look deeply at my lifelong beliefs, buried in the deep recesses of my mind, that were creating the life I was experiencing.

Over several years of therapy, I unravelled the

cocoon of beliefs which had kept me in a fog for most of my life.

What emerged rattled me, but it shepherded in the experience of freedom that I had only ever dreamed about when I was growing up.

The light-bulb moment came one day while sitting in the garden. Thoughts began to build, like clouds merging in a faraway sky.

If you wanted to groom your young daughter to protect you, how would you go about it? I found myself thinking one day.

The answer came to me almost immediately.

You'd use her as a shield because your husband who was holding a gun to your head, wouldn't shoot you with his child in front of you. Then you'd hold her close as an ally by making her sympathetic to your cause. Finally, you would erase all signs of her individuality.

Each day when I got home from school, you downloaded the day's events to ensure I was on your side. As a child, I was an unguided missile, and I could reveal 'the big secret' of what had happened in our family that night. You couldn't control your husband, or what I saw and heard. But you could control what I revealed.

As the only witness, I had to be silenced.

How do you silence someone without killing them?

My gut churned as I realised I was on the cusp of an important revelation.

You stab them in the back with words while they are acting as your shield.

How do you do that?

The thoughts now cascaded over one another, a waterfall of thoughts tumbling to their inevitable destination.

You do it by criticising and shaming everything about that child.

When that child blossomed into adolescence and wanted to look her best, Mother mocked her food choices, shamed and ridiculed her for her desire to be slim. Yet, when she gained weight as a result of doing as she was told, to "eat everything on your plate", the child was criticised for being unable to control herself, and derided as a "baby elephant".

If it wasn't my body that was criticised, it was my choice of style in clothes.

"Your bum looks too fat in that..."

"I don't like your shoes..."

"That's not what's done..."

I was the extension of a whimsical mother. She passed on to me clothes that she no longer wore so I would look more like her. (I donated them to charity).

At the end of each day, there was always the *possibility* that you would die at the hands of your husband. The helplessness I felt about that was a bottomless pit. You survived though, and the crisis came to an end.

But for me each day, there was always despair at the *certainty* that I would be shamed and humiliated. Because I could never get anything right. Shifting sands...

Just as in your marriage, Dad was the gaoler and you his prisoner, you were my gaoler and I your prisoner.

I clung to you, needing you for safety, yet at the same time, you were the enemy who was endangering my life.

Over the years, I died a thousand deaths by you, my mother, knifing me in the back, trying to kill off who I was, while at the same time I saved your life so many times.

My trauma lasted nearly fifty years.

I, Francesca, was knifed in the back every day to make sure I stayed with "two feet in one boot" so that you got to live another day.

And I couldn't breathe a word of it.

Chapter 29

How do you measure 'progress' over a lifetime, Mum?

Is it measured by the amount of money that someone accumulates?

Or is it in the technological progress we make, not as individuals but as a society? The more technologically 'advanced' we are as a society, the more 'progress' we have made as humans?

What if human progress is measured not by the sophistication of the technological gadgets we invent, or by the amount of money we make and the 'things' we accumulate, Mum, but by the value we place on a life.

If that is the measure of progress, then I would have to say that Dad did make some progress during his life despite the limitations of his Sicilian upbringing and world view.

When at the age of thirteen I told Dad that I wanted an education to year twelve and then on to university, he didn't approve, but neither did he disapprove. He just said, "You have to do the work. All I can do is work to pay the bills."

It had already been decided that Filip would attend university. Dad's tacit approval showed that in this respect, he placed as much value on his daughter's life as on his son's.

This was a huge departure from tradition for him. He told George, once, that he knew he would cop a lot of flak from your side of the family for that, but he didn't care.

By allowing me to attend university, he broke with Sicilian tradition and yes, he did cop quite a bit of flak from your father, Gaetano, and others in your family. But when the time came for the daughters of your brothers and sisters to be educated, they didn't want to be left behind. They wanted to 'keep up with the Joneses'.

Despite his limitations, and the apparent contradictions, he was a trailblazer in that respect. He only ever managed this one departure from tradition in his life though.

While you liked nice things around you, he didn't care much for all that. He considered it pretentious and ostentatious and it reminded him of those wealthy, titled men who used to piss on him back in Sicily. Paolo was a man of simple tastes. As long as he had a full belly, a roof over his head, work, a car to get around, and some money in his pocket, he was content.

But the enigma that is my father remains: Why would a man, a husband and father, be prepared to kill his wife and destroy a family in an 'honour killing'?

What terrors did this man experience that brought him to the verge of destroying so many lives? Did he feel that he might literally 'die of shame' if things did not turn out *his* way?

He took his secrets with him to the grave, and that makes me sad.

You made progress too, Mum.

Unlike many Sicilian women, you had a fighting spirit, honed through growing up with an older sister determined to keep you in your place playing second fiddle to her.

There's that hierarchy again, that pecking order, in the family.

You passed that fighting spirit on to me.

Sadly, though, when I showed that fighting spirit, you laced me up in a straitjacket.

For your own good, you told me.

But you never lost your fighting spirit. You were never a doormat to Dad, only to custom.

I just couldn't reconcile your mixture of contradictions when I was growing up.

You were conflicted yourself, weren't you?

You had imagined a much bigger, more artistic life for yourself, with dreams of being on the stage, or at the very least, going to the grand opera houses of Milan and Venice, and the great art museums of Paris, Florence, Madrid.

Delusions?

Maybe.

They remained unfulfilled *sogni*, dreams, for you for the rest of your life.

If you had stayed in Sicily, you would have fulfilled the centuries-old role for Sicilian women as custom-bearer and champion of tradition without question.

But you didn't stay there.

You moved to a big city in a progressive western country. Despite that, when you joined your husband in Australia two years after your wedding, you slowly began to realise that the dreams you had held dear for so long would be smashed.

Did you feel betrayed by your own mother and grandmothers?

Or did you just resign yourself to your fate?

Did you ever see the irony in the name you were given at birth: "*Fortunata*"?

You and Dad both gave me a life problem to solve, and because neither of you knew how to reconcile your

Sicilian upbringing with the more tolerant society in Australia, you also, unwittingly, gave me the tools to solve the problems you hadn't been able to.

Although I despised Dad for making me responsible for your life, and I hated you for making my life matter less than yours, all I can do now is to let it all go and forgive.

It is what it is. I can't turn the clock back.

The buck has to stop somewhere.

It stops with me.

Chapter 30

Early one spring morning, sitting in the garden, I watched as the sun crept over the roof of the house. The line of sunlight slid down unheralded from the upper terraces of the garden to the lower, bathing trees and flowers in warm golden light. Marvelling at this miracle of nature, I realised I had missed it all too often in my life.

Suddenly I became aware that I was simply present. I wasn't dissociating, I wasn't running away from the moment. I was in the bubble of the present, echoing with birdsong, without my gut churning, just noticing the sunlight and the plants shining in the changing light.

A thought slipped into my mind quietly, taking me by surprise.

Your life is not more important than mine. My life is important too.

Realising that it was all over, a smile stole across my face; I had detached from my history and my pain. It would no longer sabotage or predetermine my future.

I was no longer in the cage.

I was flying.

My soul was free.

Chapter 31

Resting in peace, your wrinkled hands no longer knead the bread you had made for seventy years, bread that had nourished brothers, sisters, children, grandchildren, great-grandchildren. Hands that no longer cracked olives or peeled back ripe artichokes for preserving *sott'olio*, no longer squished coarsely minced pork and fennel into sausage casings, no longer bottled the rich fragrant tomato salsa to be later transformed into a Bolognese, a napoletana, or a puttanesca.

All Souls' Day, 1st November.

Carrying a bunch of flowers and scissors, I weave my way through the graveyard towards the tomb where you rest beside dad under the monument *"Coniugi Tomasi" (Tomasi Couple)*.

Italian graves in this section of the cemetery were either in vertical above-ground family vaults, or had headstones and monuments made of granite or marble. Some were ornately decorated with sculpted monuments depicting religious iconography: statues of angels and saints, the risen Jesus, Michelangelo's *Pietà*, crucifixes.

The first time I came to this place was to buy the lease for your joint tomb, and I had been astonished. I had only ever seen a cemetery like this in Sicily: row upon row of above-ground coffins entombed in granite-clad concrete pods.

As I prepare the flowers for the vase on your grave, I look up at the headstone and recall the conversation we'd had about it. You had wanted a monument that reflected who Dad was. Even as an adult, I struggled to understand what you meant by that. I suggested something simple and dignified, but you had wanted something big, grand, and expensive, something different from the others.

"Why do you want something like that?" I asked, knowing how closely you watched every penny. "It will be much more expensive to create your artistic design in granite and marble," I continued.

"No, it has to be something big and grand, otherwise everyone will think your father didn't have enough money to buy a decent tomb. They'll think we couldn't afford something better. It's for *l'occhio sociale*, to make sure everyone knows that your father made good in this country."

I shouldn't have been surprised, but I was. The old refrain, *per l'occhio sociale,* social opinion, was the reason for the grand designs and choice building materials.

On further reflection, I realised that expensive tombs were a statement to the world about the amount of wealth, and therefore the amount of *rispettu*, to be conferred on the departed and his family. The more money they could show they had, the more respect they would be shown, as was the case in feudal Sicily, regardless of how they had come upon the wealth.

I remember telling you that it didn't matter what people thought of you after death, whether you were rich or not. But you insisted that it did.

I knew you wouldn't change your mind. This idea of doing things based on what others might think of you was so much a part of who you were, of what your culture was all about, from cradle to grave.

As I finish arranging the flowers in the vases on your joint graves, I step back and look at the whole row. A year ago the pods next to yours had been empty. Now you had a neighbour. Taking a closer look at the name sprayed in red on the naked concrete of the sealed pod, I gasped.

Then the full realisation of God's sense of humour sinks in, and I let slip an involuntary laugh.

Other mourners visiting their loved ones' graves look up to see what is so funny in such an unlikely place.

Oblivious to their disapproving sidelong glances, I stand in awe in front of the two sets of graves as the irony sank in.

Lying right beside you was your sister Antonietta's husband, Nino.

What hadn't happened in life had come to pass in death.

Your final resting place was between Nino and Dad.

Now, what would Dad think of that?

About the Author

Venera Concetta was born in Brisbane of Sicilian migrants who arrived in Australia in the aftermath of World War II. She studied psychology and ethnology at the University of Queensland, and later went on to travel widely.

Fly Francesca Fly is Venera's debut novel, but she has been writing for many years.

A self-avowed student of life, she has made the study of people negotiating change and transition the cornerstone of her professional career.

She lives just outside Brisbane where she tends her garden, writes and cooks with her grandchildren.

www.ingramcontent.com/pod-product-compliance
Lightning Source LLC
Chambersburg PA
CBHW031414240626
47154CB00001B/35